How Can Teen Pregnancy Be Reduced?

Barbara Sheen

INCONTROVERSY

ReferencePoint
Press®

San Diego, CA

© 2014 ReferencePoint Press, Inc.
Printed in the United States

For more information, contact:
ReferencePoint Press, Inc.
PO Box 27779
San Diego, CA 92198
www.ReferencePointPress.com

LIBRARY OF CONGRESS CATALOGING-IN-PUBLICATION DATA

Sheen, Barbara.
  How can teen pregnancy be reduced? / by Barbara Sheen.
    pages cm. -- (In controversy)
  Includes bibliographical references and index.
  Audience: Grade 9 to 12.
  ISBN 978-1-60152-614-4 (hardback) -- ISBN 1-60152-614-8 (hardback)
1. Teenage pregnancy--United States--Juvenile literature. 2. Teenage mothers--United States
--Juvenile literature. 3. Teenagers--Sexual behavior--United States--Juvenile literature. 4. Birth
control--United States--Juvenile literature. I. Title.
  HQ759.4.S525 2014
  306.70835--dc23
                                    2013028267

Contents

Foreword

I n 2008, as the US economy and economies worldwide were falling into the worst recession since the Great Depression, most Americans had difficulty comprehending the complexity, magnitude, and scope of what was happening. As is often the case with a complex, controversial issue such as this historic global economic recession, looking at the problem as a whole can be overwhelming and often does not lead to understanding. One way to better comprehend such a large issue or event is to break it into smaller parts. The intricacies of global economic recession may be difficult to understand, but one can gain insight by instead beginning with an individual contributing factor, such as the real estate market. When examined through a narrower lens, complex issues become clearer and easier to evaluate.

This is the idea behind ReferencePoint Press's *In Controversy* series. The series examines the complex, controversial issues of the day by breaking them into smaller pieces. Rather than looking at the stem cell research debate as a whole, a title would examine an important aspect of the debate such as *Is Stem Cell Research Necessary?* or *Is Embryonic Stem Cell Research Ethical?* By studying the central issues of the debate individually, researchers gain a more solid and focused understanding of the topic as a whole.

Each book in the series provides a clear, insightful discussion of the issues, integrating facts and a variety of contrasting opinions for a solid, balanced perspective. Personal accounts and direct quotes from academic and professional experts, advocacy groups, politicians, and others enhance the narrative. Sidebars add depth to the discussion by expanding on important ideas and events. For quick reference, a list of key facts concludes every chapter. Source notes, an annotated organizations list, bibliography, and index provide student researchers with additional tools for papers and class discussion.

The *In Controversy* series also challenges students to think critically about issues, to improve their problem-solving skills, and to sharpen their ability to form educated opinions. As President Barack Obama stated in a March 2009 speech, success in the twenty-first century will not be measurable merely by students' ability to "fill in a bubble on a test but whether they possess 21st century skills like problem-solving and critical thinking and entrepreneurship and creativity." Those who possess these skills will have a strong foundation for whatever lies ahead.

No one can know for certain what sort of world awaits today's students. What we can assume, however, is that those who are inquisitive about a wide range of issues; open-minded to divergent views; aware of bias and opinion; and able to reason, reflect, and reconsider will be best prepared for the future. As the international development organization Oxfam notes, "Today's young people will grow up to be the citizens of the future: but what that future holds for them is uncertain. We can be quite confident, however, that they will be faced with decisions about a wide range of issues on which people have differing, contradictory views. If they are to develop as global citizens all young people should have the opportunity to engage with these controversial issues."

In Controversy helps today's students better prepare for tomorrow. An understanding of the complex issues that drive our world and the ability to think critically about them are essential components of contributing, competing, and succeeding in the twenty-first century.

Why Is Teen Pregnancy a Problem?

Taylor was a typical fun-loving sixteen-year-old when she found out she was pregnant, and her life changed forever. She was stared at and ridiculed in school, and some of her friends deserted her. After her son was born, being a mother took up all of her time. "I wish I would have known how hard it would be," she explains. "Someone else's life depends on you. Having that kind of responsibility is SO stressful. I love my son with all my heart and soul, but I wish I could have waited to have him a few years. . . . Unless you are a teen mother, you don't understand how hard it is to be one."[1]

Taylor's story is not unusual. In the United States more than seven hundred thousand girls between the ages of fifteen and nineteen become pregnant each year. This translates to about thirty-four girls per thousand. Even though teen pregnancy rates are currently close to their lowest in forty years, these numbers are higher than those of any other country in the industrialized world. In comparison, teen birthrates in most European countries are below fifteen per thousand, with numbers as low as five per thousand in the Netherlands and Italy.

Teen pregnancy has a far-reaching impact. It changes the lives of young people, their families, and their offspring. It costs Ameri-

6

can taxpayers about $10 billion per year in health care costs, social programs, lost earnings, and lost tax revenue. Even though teen pregnancy rates are down, most Americans are not satisfied. As journalist Erika Christakis explains, "Winning the 'Most Improved' award isn't nearly good enough when it comes to public health issues like adolescent pregnancies. It's a bit like going from a failing grade to a D. . . . The truth is that our U.S. statistics are a comparative disaster."[2]

The Impact on Teens

Most of the costs of teen pregnancy are associated with negative consequences for young mothers. Pregnant teens are faced with the overwhelming decision of whether to terminate the pregnancy, keep the baby, or give the baby up for adoption. They may feel pressure from their parents or the baby's father to make a decision with which they are not comfortable. If the mother decides to keep the baby, she faces even more challenges. Teen mothers are less likely to finish high school than nonmothers, and they are more likely than their peers to live in poverty, depend on public assistance, and be in poor health. According to the National Campaign to Prevent Teen and Unplanned Pregnancy (NCPTUP), only 51 percent of teen mothers earn a high school diploma, compared to 89 percent of girls who do not give birth in their teens. Less than 2 percent complete college by age thirty. A lack of education makes it difficult for teen mothers to find decent-paying jobs, and it often means they will earn less for the rest of their lives.

Teen mothers who stay in school must juggle caring for a baby with studying, homework, and, often, an after-school job. This is not easy. Seventeen-year-old Darian worries about not being able to balance caring for her daughter and school. "I don't sleep a lot and she has to go everywhere with me,"[3] she says. Moreover, most teen mothers get little help from their baby's father. About 80 percent of teen fathers do not marry the mother of their baby, and they pay less than eight hundred dollars a year in child support.

Babies born to teen parents also face negative consequences.

Two teens ponder the prospects of a positive pregnancy test. US teen pregnancy rates have significantly decreased over the past forty years, but they continue to exceed levels found in other industrialized nations.

They are less likely to receive adequate prenatal care, which puts them at risk for low birth weight, a condition that is often accompanied by serious health issues like cerebral palsy, deafness, and respiratory problems. According to the March of Dimes, babies born to teenage mothers are more likely to die during their first year of life than babies born to older mothers. The younger the mother is, the higher the risk.

The children of teen mothers are also at risk of growing up in poverty. The Annie E. Casey Foundation, an organization dedicated to helping at-risk youths, reports that "the poverty rate for children born to teenage mothers who have never married and who did not graduate from high school is 78 percent. This compares to 9 percent of children born to women over age 20 who are currently married and did graduate from high school."[4]

Moreover, babies born to women seventeen or younger are more likely to be abused or neglected and to wind up in foster care than the offspring of women aged twenty or older, possibly because teens lack parenting skills. When compared to other children, children of teen mothers are more likely to do poorly in school. Daughters of teen mothers are three times as likely to become teen mothers themselves, and sons are more likely to wind up incarcerated.

A Ripple Effect

Although teen pregnancy is a personal matter, it has a significant economic impact on society. Approximately 80 percent of teen parents depend on government assistance in the form of welfare, food stamps, Medicaid, and other social programs. This costs taxpayers about $5 billion annually. That number does not include the cost of loss of revenue due to lower taxes paid by teen mothers throughout their lifetimes because of lower education and earnings. Nor does it include the cost to individual states, which varies due to the state's population, the incidence of teen childbearing, and participation in publicly funded programs. For example, in 2008 (according to the most recent figures available) the cost ranged from $16 million in North Dakota to $1.2 billion in Texas.

Teen pregnancy has a ripple effect that impacts individuals and society. According to a 2012 nationwide survey conducted by the NCPTUP, nine out of ten adults and teens who answered the survey believe that teen pregnancy is an important issue, even compared to other economic and social issues facing the country.

Numerous efforts have been made to address the issue of teen pregnancy. However, there is still no definitive solution to the problem. Is sex education in schools the answer? If so, how

> "The poverty rate for children born to teenage mothers who have never married and who did not graduate from high school is 78 percent."[4]
>
> — Annie E. Casey Foundation, an organization dedicated to helping at-risk youths.

should it be taught? Does access to birth control help, and should parents be involved? What role should the media play? What can parents and communities do? Do programs that change teen attitudes work? Differing groups have conflicting answers to these questions, but the consensus is that something must be done.

Facts

- According to the NCPTUP, girls who have a baby at seventeen or younger can expect to earn $28,000 less in the fifteen years following the birth than if they had delayed childbearing until they were twenty.

- Studies have found that the children of teen mothers are more likely to be held back a grade level, score lower on standardized tests, and drop out of high school than children born to mothers age twenty or older.

- According to Find Youth Info, a US government website, teen fathers are 25 to 30 percent less likely to graduate from high school than their peers.

- According to the Centers for Disease Control and Prevention (CDC), the children of teen mothers are more likely to be unemployed or underemployed as young adults than the children of older mothers.

What Are the Origins of Concerns About Teen Pregnancy?

In 1962 Judi Loren Grace was fifteen years old and pregnant. At that time, pregnant teens were treated like pariahs. They were typically kicked out of school and fired from jobs. Many were forced to marry. Those who did not marry were often sent to group homes for unwed mothers, where their pregnancy was hidden. Once they gave birth, their babies were usually given up for adoption. "If you got pregnant you had two choices; you either had a shotgun wedding or you went to a home," Grace explains. "You had to go there and hide . . . and after you had your baby, you went out the door and were never heard from again. And then you returned home and you pretended that nothing ever happened."[5]

Teen pregnancy is not a modern phenomenon. How it is dealt with, and the focus of concern, however, have changed. Until the late 1960s, society was more concerned about a pregnant woman's marital status than her age. Premarital sex was regarded as immoral, and unwed mothers were considered social delinquents. Society expected pregnant women of all ages to wed, and most did. Those who did not were pressured to give their babies up for adoption. As changes in society made premarital sex more acceptable, single parenthood became more common. Because many teen mothers were not able to support themselves and looked to society for assistance, public concern shifted to a pregnant woman's age. With this shift, teen pregnancy became a controversial issue due to differences in the way social liberals and conservatives viewed the problem and its solution.

The First Sexual Revolution

Many things have changed during the past one hundred years, including dating practices. At the turn of the twentieth century, a date was a formal event supervised by a chaperone. Sexual activity outside of marriage was considered indecent. Respectable people did not talk about sex or care about sexual fulfillment. Early marriage was common. Once young people reached puberty, they were considered adults. It was not unusual for couples to marry and start families in their midteens or for young girls to marry older men and bear them children.

Cultural changes during the 1920s had a major effect on the lives of adolescents. With World War I a memory, Americans were in a celebratory mood and began to let go of some of their sexual inhibitions. The idea that sexual fulfillment was part of a happy marriage became popular. Dating practices became less formal; for the first time, couples went out without a chaperone. The passage of Prohibition, which banned the sale of alcoholic beverages, led to the establishment of secret clubs known as speakeasies, where liquor was served and amorous feeling often intensified. Rather than suppress these feelings, the growing popularity of the automobile gave couples a private place for sexual activity. Teen pregnancy became more common, with birthrates reaching about fifty births per one thousand during the 1920s. Since almost all of these pregnancies were accompanied by marriage, society remained unconcerned. An increase in sexually transmitted diseases (STDs), however, did cause concern. In

Two couples happily sample homemade beer around 1925. Societal restrictions on drinking, dating, and sex eased during the 1920s as Americans celebrated the end of World War I.

response, many high schools added sex education classes to the curriculum. These classes taught students that sexual experimentation before marriage endangered their health.

Early Marriage as a Way to Manage Teen Sexuality

The sexual revolution of the 1920s was seen by some reformers as an indication of the moral decline of American society. When the Great Depression of the 1930s hit, the celebratory atmosphere

The Comstock Act

The Comstock Act was an 1873 anti-obscenity law that made it a federal offense to distribute obscene material and objects of immoral use through the US mail or across state lines. Under the Comstock Act, contraceptives were defined as obscene and illicit material, making the distribution of contraceptives, information about contraceptives, and advertisements for contraceptives through the mail or across state lines punishable by imprisonment. The act also banned distribution of information about abortion.

Soon after the federal law was passed, twenty-four states passed their own versions of the law, restricting distribution and use of contraceptives in their state. Some of the strictest laws were passed in New England. In Connecticut, for example, married couples could be arrested for using contraceptives in the privacy of their own home. That particular law was rarely enforced. However, when birth control activists attempted to distribute contraceptives in public forums, they were usually arrested. The Comstock Act was amended to delete all mention of contraception in 1971.

and sexual freedom of the 1920s faded. Not long after, public attention fixed on World War II. With so many men fighting overseas, pregnancy rates decreased. When the war ended, however, things changed significantly.

Returning troops were eager to reconnect with the girls they left behind. In the decade following the war's end, teen birthrates, like all American birthrates, increased dramatically. According to the NCPTUP, between 1940 and 1957 the number of teenage girls giving birth increased by 78 percent. By 1957 birthrates among teens aged fifteen to nineteen reached a high of ninety-six per one thousand. Most of these pregnant teens married shortly after the pregnancy occurred. So-called shotgun weddings were common.

These were weddings forced on one or both of the participants in order to protect the reputations of the pregnant girl and her family. Indeed, many women had sex with their boyfriends with the understanding that marriage would follow. As author Frank F. Furstenberg Jr. explains, "Pregnancy was often part of the courtship process, propelling many young couples into marriage at an accelerated pace. Women risked their reputations when they consented to have sex. If they were unlucky enough to get pregnant, their boyfriends were expected to do the honorable thing—which they usually did, whether willingly or reluctantly."[6]

Although unwed motherhood was socially unacceptable and women who engaged in casual sex were considered immoral, as long as pregnant teens married, society looked the other way. Marriage served the interest of society. It was a way to control teen sexuality. And, since husbands were expected to support their families but single mothers often depended on public assistance, marriage provided a solution to what would otherwise be a costly social problem.

Pregnant Teens Had Few Options

Some pregnant teens, however, did not marry. These young women had few options. Unwed mothers and their children were social outcasts. Rather than become an unwed mother, some girls had illegal abortions. Others spent most of their pregnancy in a group home for unwed mothers or at the home of an out-of-town relative. This allowed their families to hide the pregnancy from society. The girls were hidden until they gave birth, at which time great pressure was placed on them to give their babies up for adoption. In order to convince them to do so, they were often made to feel guilty and unworthy of motherhood. As women's health activist Wendy McCarthy explains, "One of the things that's really hard for people to imagine now is how tough it was . . . , because the penalties of an unplanned pregnancy were public shame and humiliation, estrangement from your family, facing a termination of pregnancy, or continuing with the pregnancy and adopting the baby."[7]

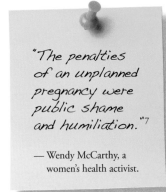

"The penalties of an unplanned pregnancy were public shame and humiliation."[7]

— Wendy McCarthy, a women's health activist.

"Make Love, Not War"

Up until the mid-1960s, unwed motherhood remained stigmatized. Teen pregnancy stayed a nonissue as long as young mothers married. However, as the decade progressed, attitudes toward sexuality changed. Premarital sex and unwed motherhood became more common, raising the issue of teen pregnancy.

The 1960s was a period of social upheaval characterized by the war in Vietnam, the civil rights and women's liberation movements, sit-ins and love-ins, the creation of the birth control pill, experiments in communal living, overt use of psychedelic drugs, and open sexuality. Throughout the decade, young people challenged traditional values. The slogan "Make love, not war" became their battle cry, and promiscuity and casual sex became the norm. Events like the Be-in in San Francisco in 1967, which featured illicit drugs, rock music, public nudity, and casual sex, typified the new sexual freedom. Claudia King, who was there, recalls, "You might see people making love on the street corner and have to walk around them and say 'Hmm, hmm.' It was just, I mean, it was out there!"[8]

Despite the new sexual freedom, teens had difficulty obtaining contraceptives. Ironically, even though the birth control pill first became available in 1960, restrictive laws in many states made it illegal for unmarried females to obtain the pill or other birth control devices. Indeed, in 1967 birth control rights activist Bill Baird was arrested and jailed for three months for giving a condom and contraceptive foam to a female student at Boston University.

Limited access to birth control, however, did not stop young people from being sexually active. And, as the stigma of premarital sex lessened, so did the urgency for pregnant teens to marry. By the late 1960s, single motherhood had become more common. Faced with limited incomes and the cost of raising a child, many of these young mothers depended on public assistance and social programs for support. As Americans became more aware of the problem, concern grew. A 1968 report by sociologist Arthur Campbell that focused on the impact of teen pregnancy brought the issue into the forefront. Campbell wrote:

> The girl who has an illegitimate child at the age of 16 suddenly has 90 percent of her life's script written for her. She will probably drop out of school; even if someone else in her family helps to take care of the baby, she will probably not be able to find a steady job that pays enough to provide for herself and her child. . . . Her life choices are few, and most of them are bad.[9]

In response to what was now seen as a problem, a group of concerned educators founded the Sexuality Information and Education Council of the United States (SIECUS). SIECUS worked

"The girl who has an illegitimate child at the age of 16 suddenly has 90 percent of her life's script written for her."[9]

— Arthur Campbell, a sociologist.

with school districts to change the content of sex education classes to include information about sexual intercourse, contraception, and pregnancy. By the end of the 1960s, 50 percent of American high schools followed the SIECUS model.

An Epidemic

Although teen birthrates fell from 89.1 per 1,000 to 51.5 per 1,000 between 1960 and 1978, public concern grew. These numbers did not tell the whole story. Birthrates were down among women ages eighteen and nineteen, but they were up among females seventeen and younger. Most troubling was that birthrates among ten- to fourteen-year-olds increased by 33.3 percent. The idea of such young girls bearing and raising children inflamed the public.

By 1977 teenagers accounted for 48.3 percent of all out-of-wedlock births in the United States. The burden these young mothers placed on society added to public worry. According to an estimate by the Urban Institute, a Washington, DC, think tank that conducts research, in 1975 the federal government paid about $4.75 billion in Aid to Families with Dependent Children (AFDC) to women who had their first child while a teenager. This amounted to more than half of AFDC spending for that year and did not include other programs, such as food stamps, Medicaid, or state costs.

Filled with a sense of urgency, policy makers in Washington declared teen pregnancy an epidemic. As Maris Vinovskis, the deputy staff director of the House Select Committee on Population, explained, "Almost everyone in Washington assumed that the problem of adolescent pregnancy was a very serious social and health crisis that necessitated an immediate response. . . . Therefore, policy-makers usually advocated drastic and immediate steps to deal with this unprecedented situation."[10]

Responding to the problem, Congress passed the Adolescent Health Services and Pregnancy Prevention and Care Act in 1978. The goal, according to lawyer and reproductive health advocate Cynthia Dallard, was "to prevent unwanted early and repeat preg-

"Almost everyone in Washington assumed that the problem of adolescent pregnancy was a very serious social and health crisis that necessitated an immediate response."[10]

— Maris Vinovskis, the former deputy staff director of the House Select Committee on Population.

Margaret Sanger

Margaret Sanger (1879–1966) was an American activist who devoted her life to making birth control available to women. Sanger coined the term *birth control*, opened the first birth control clinic in the United States, and established Planned Parenthood. Sanger's interest in birth control arose from personal experience. Her mother had twenty-two pregnancies in eighteen years. When her mother died at age fifty, Sanger blamed her father. "You caused this," she told him. "Mother is dead from having too many children."

Sanger felt that in order to live healthy lives, women needed to control their fertility. Therefore, in 1914 she began distributing information about birth control. In 1915 she sent a birth control device through the mail. At the time, sending contraceptives through the mail was illegal, and she was arrested. When she opened the first birth control clinic in the United States in 1916, she was arrested again. The arrests did not deter her. In 1921 she founded the American Birth Control League, which later became Planned Parenthood. She spent the rest of her life working to make birth control accessible to American women. Much of what has been accomplished is due to her efforts.

Quoted in PBS, "The Pill: People & Events: Margaret Sanger (1879–1966)." www.pbs.org.

nancies and to help adolescents become productive, independent contributors to family and community life."[11] The act established the Office of Adolescent Pregnancy Programs to coordinate eighty-five federal programs aimed at preventing teen pregnancy and to provide support services to teen mothers and their children.

Morality vs. Social Concerns

By 1980 the federal government had spent $200 million on teen pregnancy prevention and support services. Moreover, in 1978

Congress had amended the Federal Family Planning Act (Title X), which provided funds for family-planning clinics like the Planned Parenthood Federation of America, which provided free or low-cost contraceptive services and other reproductive health care to women. Up until 1978 the clinics did not provide services to unwed minors. That year, however, the government mandated that the clinics serve women of all ages, no matter their marital status, which gave unwed teens access to birth control.

Not everyone was happy with the new social agenda. A number of conservative Christians objected to it on religious grounds. They questioned the morality of social programs that recognized premarital sex as the norm, gave unmarried minors access to contraceptives, and provided public assistance to single mothers. They also condemned the legalization of abortion by a 1973 US Supreme Court ruling. In 1979, under the leadership of the Reverend Jerry Falwell, these opponents formed a group known as the Moral Majority, which pressured lawmakers to restore morality to the nation by applying their interpretation of Christian teachings to social issues and public policy. The Moral Majority quickly became a rising force in the Republican Party, helping elect President Ronald Reagan in 1980 and 1984, and President George H.W. Bush in 1988. As political commentator Pat Buchanan explains, "What Jerry Falwell did, he became the voice and face of a Christian conservative movement, which . . . was defending its own values, convictions and beliefs, which it saw under sudden and massive assault. And he organized this movement that already existed and pointed it in a political direction, and he was a striking success."[12]

Political Backlash

The influence of the Moral Majority and other Christian conservative groups was felt throughout the 1980s and early 1990s. Philosophical differences between conservatives, who viewed teen pregnancy as evidence of the moral breakdown of society, and liberals, who viewed teen pregnancy as a public health and social welfare matter, made the issue of teen pregnancy controversial. Both groups wanted to reduce teen pregnancy, but their approaches were very different. Social liberals believed that sex education

What Should Schools Teach About Sex?

I
n 2011 ninety girls enrolled at Frayser High School in Memphis, Tennessee, became pregnant. This constituted 18 percent of the school's female students. High pregnancy rates at Frayser, as well as in other schools in Tennessee, are not unusual. According to the National Center for Health Statistics, in 2013 Tennessee ranked ninth in the nation for teen pregnancy, and Shelby County, where Frayser High School is located, ranked first in Tennessee. Some individuals, including Terrika Sutton, a sixteen-year-old mother and student at Frayser, think many of these pregnancies could have been prevented through more effective sex education. "It's a shame that all these girls at Frayser are pregnant, but it ain't nothing new," Terrika explains. "They need a class where they teach the girls before they get pregnant to use protection and stuff."[17]

Claudia Haltom, the head of A Step Ahead Foundation, an organization that provides free birth control to women in Shelby County, agrees. She believes young people need more information about sex in order to make wise decisions. "Knowledge is power," she says. "When kids understand how their bodies work, they behave responsibly. When they don't have knowledge, their level of responsibility is sometimes questionable."[18]

> "When kids understand how their bodies work, they behave responsibly."[18]
>
> — Claudia Haltom, the head of A Step Ahead Foundation.

Others have a different point of view. According to a Fox News survey of nine hundred Americans on the topic of sex education, 20 percent of those who answered the survey think that sex education has no place in schools. Many individuals with this point of view are Christian conservatives. They are concerned that what is taught in sex education challenges their personal morals. In their opinion, sex education should be taught at home so that parents can impart their own values to their children. As Utah senator Stuart Reid explains, "To replace the parent in the school setting, among people who we have no idea what their morals are, we have no idea what their values are, yet we turn our children over to them to instruct them in the most sensitive sexual activities in their lives, I think is wrongheaded."[19]

A Contentious Topic

Many Americans disagree. In a 2012 national survey by Planned Parenthood, 93 percent of respondents said that sex education should be taught in high school. In answer to another question, 84 percent of survey participants said it should actually begin in middle school. However, the curriculum of such courses remains controversial. In general, social conservatives support abstinence-based sex education, which teaches that chastity is the only way to prevent pregnancy. Lessons stress the value of waiting until marriage to have sex. Until then, students are instructed to "just say no." Advocates maintain that when young people are taught that abstaining from sex is the only healthy and morally correct option, they will live up to the standard set for them.

> "It's crucial that teens have information about both contraception and abstinence."[20]
>
> — Debra Hauser, the president of Advocates for Youth.

Many social liberals feel differently. They insist that it is unrealistic to expect young people to abstain from having sex until marriage. Therefore, in order to prevent unplanned early pregnancies, sex education should be comprehensive, instructing students on all aspects of human sexuality, including contraception. "We have to be honest with ourselves, 95 percent of Americans are going to have sex before marriage, and it's crucial that teens have information about both contraception and abstinence,"[20] says Debra Hauser, presi-

dent of Advocates for Youth, an organization that champions comprehensive sexual education. She goes on to say that comprehensive sex education gives young people the tools to make safe choices.

Many Questions

Federal law does not require schools to provide sexual education. According to the National Conference of State Legislatures, as of 2013 twenty-two states and the District of Columbia require sex education in public schools. In the remaining states, local school districts decide whether to provide sex education. Parents can opt out of sex education classes on their children's behalf in thirty-three states, and three states require signed parental permission for students to participate in the classes.

Whether abstinence-based or comprehensive sex education is taught depends on individual states and local school districts. The curriculum usually reflects local values. As reporter Molly Masland

A Tennessee teen who became pregnant while a senior in high school feeds her five-month-old daughter. Tennessee was ranked ninth in the nation for teen pregnancies in 2013.

explains, "In some states, such as Louisiana, kids might learn about HIV/AIDS, but not about any other STDs or how to prevent pregnancy. In other states, like Washington, teens receive information on everything from birth control pills to homosexuality."[21]

At what grade level sex education begins, how often classes are held, and who teaches the classes are also a state and/or local decision. Many school districts begin sex education instruction in fifth grade as a part of health education. Others do not offer instruction until high school. A few begin in kindergarten. In 2013 Chicago's board of education passed a new policy that requires all students to receive 300 minutes per year of medically accurate, age-appropriate sex education in kindergarten through fourth grade and 675 minutes in grades five through twelve. In the younger grades, instruction focuses on families, human anatomy, and reproduction. Instruction for older students focuses on the transmission and prevention of STIs, reproduction, and contraception. Beginning sex education in kindergarten has its supporters and opponents. Parent Melissa Diebold finds the concept disturbing. "I don't think its age appropriate," she contends. "They have no concept of anything like that [sexuality] at that stage in life."[22]

Hauser disagrees:

Quality sex education should start in kindergarten. Early elementary school students need to learn the proper names for their body parts, the difference between good touch and bad touch, and ways in which they can be a good friend (the foundation for healthy intimate relationships later in life). Fourth- and fifth-graders need information about puberty and their changing bodies, Internet safety, and the harmful impact of bullying. And seventh-, eighth- and ninth-graders are ready for information about body image, reproduction, abstinence, contraception, H.I.V. and disease prevention, communication, and the topic they most want to learn about: healthy relationships.[23]

Who teaches sex education classes, and how often classes are held, also varies. Some school districts provide students with twenty to forty-five hours of sex education per year beginning in

Sexually Transmitted Infections

An important goal of both comprehensive and abstinence-based sex education is preventing HIV and other STDs. Both curriculums teach that infections can be transmitted from one person to another through sexual intercourse, oral sex, or anal sex. Infections that are transmitted through sexual activity (STIs) can become sexually transmitted diseases (or STDs) over time. Two other types of infections—the human papilloma virus (HPV) and genital ulcers—can also be transmitted through skin-to-skin contact with infected areas. People can be infected with an STI without showing any symptoms, but they can still pass on the infection.

STIs can be caused by bacteria, fungus, parasites, or a virus. Some infections are incurable, which makes prevention vital. Both comprehensive sex education and abstinence-based lessons stress that the most effective way to prevent the transmission of STIs is to avoid the exchange of bodily fluids or skin-to-skin contact with infected sores. Comprehensive sex education also teaches that using a condom during sexual intercourse is the next best prevention method. It limits exposure and greatly reduces the risk of contracting an infection.

University of Georgia analyzed teen pregnancy rates in states that emphasize abstinence education. They wanted to find out if these states had lower teen pregnancy rates than other states. After analyzing data from every state, the researchers found that teen pregnancy rates were highest in those states where abstinence-based sex education was emphasized and lowest in states where contraceptive use was stressed. For example, teen birthrates in Mississippi, where abstinence-based education is the norm, are fifty births per one thousand girls, compared to thirteen births per one thousand in New Hampshire, where comprehensive sex education is the norm. According to study coauthor Kathryn Stanger-Hall, "If abstinence education reduced teen pregnancy as proponents claim, the correlation would be in the opposite direction."[29]

One reason for these results may be that sexually active teens who receive abstinence-based instruction are less likely than other teens to use contraceptives, raising their risk of unintended pregnancy. As Johns Hopkins researcher Janet Rosenbaum explains, "This may be because they were taught about the disadvantages of condoms in abstinence based education classes. Since such programs promote abstinence only, they tend to give only the disadvantages of birth control. . . . People end up thinking you may as well not bother using birth control or condoms."[30]

One area in which abstinence-based instruction appears to be successful is in influencing preteens and young teenagers to delay sexual activity. A 2010 University of Pennsylvania study compared the sexual activity of 662 sixth and seventh graders. The students attended either an abstinence-based class; a safe-sex class, which covered contraception; a combined abstinence and safe-sex class; or a health-promotion control group. Researchers found that two-thirds of the students who attended the abstinence-based class delayed sexual activity for two years, in contrast with one-half of the other subjects.

Comprehensive Sexual Education

Critics of abstinence-based sexual education point to comprehensive sexual education as a better alternative. Though programs differ, comprehensive sexual education typically provides lessons on abstinence, human sexuality, obtaining and using birth control, abortion, the transmission and prevention of STDs, and sexual orientation. Classes often include sexually explicit discussions and hands-on activities like putting a condom on a banana. Programs are based on scientific facts and are supported by many medical and public health groups, including the American Medical Association (AMA) and the National Institutes of Health. Comprehensive sex education is also supported by many Americans. According to a 2012 survey by the NCPTUP, 49 percent of teens and 74 percent of adults who answered the survey desired teens to be educated about both abstinence and contraceptives rather than one or the other. As of 2013 nineteen states require sex education to be medically accurate, and seventeen states and the District of Columbia require information on contraceptives be provided.

Supporters of comprehensive sex education maintain that it gives teens the tools they need to avoid unplanned pregnancies and STDs. As Jessica Sheets of the NCPTUP maintains, "Teen pregnancy is 100% preventable. You never have to have another pregnant teen if they know how to protect themselves from pregnancy either by waiting or by using contraception correctly every single time they have sex."[31]

How Effective Is Comprehensive Sex Education?

Opponents say comprehensive sex education normalizes casual sex, leading to risky behavior and sexual experimentation among teens. Organizations including the Heritage Foundation and the NAEA argue that comprehensive sex education condones teen sex. In their opinion, the primary focus of comprehensive sex education is the promotion of safe sex rather than providing young people with the tools for making good decisions and avoiding unnecessary risks. The safe-sex message, these groups believe, gives young people the impression that being sexually active is acceptable as long as they use a condom or other form of birth control. This creates a false sense of security, making it more likely that they will take part in risky activities such as initiating sex at a young age and/or having casual sex with multiple partners.

Despite these objections, studies of comprehensive sex education programs indicate a different result. An Advocates for Youth study examined the behavioral outcomes of twenty-three comprehensive sex education programs and found that teens who participated in the programs demonstrated statistically significant delays in the initiation of sex, fewer sex partners, a decrease in the incidence of unprotected sex, and statistically significant increases in the use of condoms and other contraceptives.

Moreover, comprehensive sex education appears to be more

"You never have to have another pregnant teen if they know how to protect themselves from pregnancy."[31]

— Jessica Sheets
assistant director of
dommunications of the
NCPTUP.

A New Jersey health educator removes the thirty-five pound empathy belly from a student who took part in a program that promotes safe sex. A realistic view of pregnancy can get teens to think carefully about becoming sexually active or, at the very least, about having unprotected sex.

effective in reducing teen pregnancy than abstinence-based education. Researchers at ETR Associates in California analyzed and compared the results of eighty-three studies that measured the impact of different sex education programs on the sexual behavior of young people ages fifteen to nineteen. The researchers found that teens who received comprehensive sex education were 50 percent less likely to become pregnant or cause a pregnancy than those who received abstinence-only education. The CDC attributes the current forty-year-low rate of teen pregnancy to increased use of condoms and other forms of birth control, which may be related to comprehensive sex education's emphasis on safe sex. As Amber, a teen advocate for comprehensive sex education, points out, "If teens are taught no sex is safe sex, they'll have sex anyway without knowing the right thing to do. . . . Teach teens how to have safer sex. Using condoms and birth control will help a majority of young people."[32]

Simulating Pregnancy and Parenthood

Many schools supplement both abstinence-based and comprehensive sexual education lessons with programs that simulate pregnancy and parenthood. In family science classes across the United States, it is common for male and female students to be given a 30-pound (14 kg) bag, which they wear hanging from their midsection for a school day. The bag, which is known as an empathy belly, mimics the stress that pregnancy places on the body. Among other features, most bags contain suspended weights that imitate fetal movement and a bladder pouch filled with warm water that simulates the way a fetus's head presses on a pregnant woman's bladder, making her need to urinate. At first many students think wearing the belly is fun, but reality soon sets in. After a day spent repeatedly sitting in and rising from chairs, bending down, walking from class to class carrying extra weight, and frequently running to the bathroom, teens realize how physically uncomfortable pregnancy can be and how it can alter their lives. Lily, a family science student, explains:

> In the beginning I thought it was fun, but by the end of the day I was really done "being pregnant." . . . I learned that carrying the extra weight of a baby is not enjoyable and can hurt your back, and that being pregnant really does make you go to the bathroom all the time. Also, I wasn't able to fit in the normal desks and had to wear an extra large t-shirt. By the end of the day it was very hard to focus because I was so tired and somewhat cranky.[33]

Caring for lifelike dolls programmed to cry at realistic intervals is also part of many school pregnancy prevention campaigns. Students take care of the dolls for at least twenty-four hours, which is not as easy as it sounds. The dolls cry like real babies at intervals ranging from every fifteen minutes to once every few hours. The teens are given a key that they insert into the doll for a specific length of time (lasting from five to thirty minutes) to simulate feeding, bathing, diaper changing, and comforting the doll. A computer chip inside the doll tracks how well students do these tasks. Students commonly complain about losing sleep, missing social events, and being unable to study because they had to care for the crying dolls. The goal of the activity is to make teens aware of the heavy responsibility of parenthood. After caring for the dolls, it is not unusual for students to say that they plan to wait to become parents.

Schools Are Taking Steps

Schools across America are taking steps to confront the issue of teen pregnancy. How they deal with the problem depends on state and local values. Every program has its supporters and opponents as well as its advantages and disadvantages. Although some strategies appear to be more effective than others, teen pregnancy remains a problem. That is why some individuals feel that providing teenagers access to contraceptives may be the answer.

Facts

- Between 1996 and 2009 the federal government spent $1.5 billion on abstinence-based sexual education programs.

- According to the National Center for Health Statistics (NCHS), New Hampshire, Massachusetts, Connecticut, and Vermont (each of which provide comprehensive sex education) have the lowest teen pregnancy rates in the United States, with rates under seventeen per one thousand.

- According to the NCHS, Arkansas and Mississippi (both of which focus on abstinence-based sex education) have the highest teen pregnancy rates in the United States, with rates of about fifty per one thousand.

Should Teens Have Access to Birth Control?

Ninety-five percent of teens who answered a 2012 survey conducted by the NCPTUP said that it is important that they avoid getting pregnant or getting someone else pregnant. The best way for sexually active people to avoid pregnancy is to consistently use contraception.

Encouraging the Use of Contraceptives

Although use of contraceptives among teens has increased since the 2000s, the Guttmacher Institute reports that approximately 19 percent of sexually active females ages fifteen to nineteen and 20 percent of males ages fifteen to nineteen do not use contraceptives regularly. There are a number of reasons why this is so. Teens report not using contraceptives because they are too embarrassed to bring the subject up with their parents, doctor, or sex partner. Some report the problem is lack of confidential access to birth control.

Being insufficiently educated about sex, contraception, and pregnancy is also a top reason. A 2012 CDC study found that of five thousand pregnant teens, one-third reported not using contraceptives because they did not think they could get pregnant. Many of these young women believed that contraceptives do not work. Some thought that being virgins protected them from becoming pregnant. In reality, teenagers who do not use contraceptives the first time they have sex are twice as likely to become pregnant as those who use contraceptives. As Bill Albert, a spokesperson for the NCPTUP, says, "Not to get too biological here, but the only teen girls getting pregnant are the ones who are having sex and not using contraception, carefully, or at all."[34]

In an attempt to increase contraceptive use among sexually active teens, some schools have established school-based health clinics that distribute condoms. Health care agencies such as Planned Parenthood and the Family Planning Council (FPC) also provide teens with birth control.

The issue of whether teens should have access to contraceptives and whether that access should be confidential or involve their parents or guardians is a source of heated argument in the United States. In general, public opinion is divided along political lines. Social conservatives insist that teenagers are too young to make medical decisions that can jeopardize their general well-being without parental input. Social liberals point out that an American's constitutional right to privacy gives teens the legal right to obtain and use birth control products without parental notification or permission.

Clinical psychologist Ana Nogales explains the issue in this way:

A boy (or girl) can walk into any drug store and buy a package of condoms with no problem. But a girl needs a doctor's prescription to procure birth control pills or any other female contraceptive product. Even though she can legally do so without informing her parents, do her parents still have a responsibility to make sure she makes the right decisions about her sex life? Or would that be an invasion of her privacy?[35]

Who Controls a Teen's Body?

The question of who controls a teen's body—teens or their parents or guardians—is a basic part of the issue of whether minors should have access to birth control, and, if so, whether such access should

be confidential. In the United States each state has different laws about whether minors can get prescription contraceptives without involving a parent. Federal laws currently require that health care services funded by Title X, a federal program that provides money for family planning clinics, and Medicaid, a federal program that pays for health services for low-income individuals, must treat all patients confidentially, including teens. If teens seek contraceptives from other sources, such as private doctors or state-funded clinics, state law applies. State laws usually reflect local values. Currently twenty-one states and the District of Columbia allow minors to obtain contraception without parental knowledge. Another twenty-five states permit minors confidential access to contraceptives under one or more circumstances. These include being married, being a parent, having graduated from high school, having previously been pregnant, or having a physician's referral. Four states have no explicit policy.

Anyone of any age can buy condoms with no questions asked and without a prescription, but sexually active teens are not always willing to buy them. So some school-based clinics distribute condoms to students.

Despite federal requirements, some lawmakers—particularly those supported by conservative constituents—are trying to pass state laws that mandate parental consent for federally funded contraceptive services. They maintain that, under the law, parents have the right to make medical decisions concerning minor children. Therefore, they should be involved in reproductive health decisions involving their minor children, especially since some forms of birth control present potential health risks. According to Leslee J. Unruh, president of the Abstinence Clearinghouse, "From birth, parents are responsible for helping their children to grow, to learn, and to succeed. Why is it that as soon as children become teenagers, the ability of parents to help their children is suddenly not good enough. . . . Our children deserve better. They deserve the help and direction parents can provide in making life-altering decisions as adolescents."[36]

Thus far the courts have ruled against requiring parental notification for federally funded contraceptive services. Many Americans applaud these rulings. Says one teen mom, "Had I been able to obtain birth control without my mom, or God forbid, my dad, I may not be in this situation. . . . Teens have sex. . . . At least make sure they're safe and protected when doing it."[37]

It is not known how many parents are aware that their children are receiving sexual health services or how mandatory parental notification would affect teens. A study by the Guttmacher Institute, which surveyed a national sample of teenage girls who were obtaining prescription birth control from federally funded family planning clinics, found that 60 percent of the girls who answered the survey said that their parents knew they were visiting the clinics. Fifty-nine percent of these girls said they would continue to get contraceptives at the clinic even if parental notification was required. On the other hand, of the young women whose parents did not know they were visiting the clinics, 70 percent said they would stop using prescription birth control if parental notification were required. Of these girls, 18 percent said they would remain sexually active but practice unsafe sex.

"From birth, parents are responsible for helping their children to grow, to learn, and to succeed. Why is it that as soon as children become teenagers, the ability of parents to help their children is suddenly not good enough?"[36]

— Leslee J. Unruh, president of the Abstinence Clearinghouse.

Access to Condoms

Even in cases when teens do not have confidential access to prescription birth control, it is relatively easy for them to obtain condoms. Condoms are sold over the counter (no prescription needed) throughout the United States. They are usually displayed on open racks in supermarkets, drugstores, and convenience stores. Anyone, no matter their age, can buy condoms, no questions asked.

School Clinics Offer Birth Control

In addition to dispensing condoms, some school health clinics make other methods of birth control available to students. More than fifty school health clinics in New York City dispense the morning-after pill. The clinics also provide prescriptions for birth control pills, intrauterine devices, hormone-delivering injections, and birth control patches.

The policy has raised a lot of controversy. Although some schools allow parents to opt their children out of the program by signing a form, some do not. Some parents feel that these schools are overstepping their authority. Moreover, it is not uncommon for students who do not want their parents to know they are sexually active to withhold the opt-out form from their parents. As one Brooklyn high school junior who was administered the morning-after pill in school told the *New York Times*, "My mom, she doesn't even know they have this stuff."

On the other hand, many parents are grateful that the services exist. According to Dr. Angela Diaz, who runs three New York high school clinics, "They wish their kids would talk to them, but given the reality, they're happy there is a place where they can be helped."

Quoted in Anemona Hartocollis and Michaelle Bond, "Ready Access to Plan B Pills in City Schools," *New York Times*, July 11, 2013. www.nytimes.com.

Yet this was not always the case. In the past condoms were kept behind pharmacy counters. Buying a box was an embarrassing experience for nervous teens. It was not easy for teens to face an often judgmental pharmacist who, in small communities, probably knew their parents. Many embarrassed teens fled without making a purchase; others, like the teen in the film *American Graffiti,* wound up buying a stack of unneeded toiletries before getting up the courage to ask for condoms.

It is somewhat easier for modern teens to purchase condoms, and condom use by teenagers has increased. A 2012 survey sponsored by the CDC found that 80 percent of the sexually active teenage boys who answered the survey used condoms, compared to 72 percent in 2002.

School Health Clinics

Even though getting condoms at stores is no longer difficult, many teens would rather obtain them in a more discreet environment. More than thirteen hundred American schools have school-based health clinics where students have free, confidential access to condoms and sometimes other forms of birth control. The clinics are usually staffed by a school nurse or other health care professional. Some clinics are equipped with free condom dispensers placed right in the doorway of the health clinic so that students can get condoms without being monitored. About 2 million students use these clinics. Seventeen-year-old Denise is an example. When she and her boyfriend decided to become sexually active, she turned to her school health clinic for help. The nurse supplied her with a box of condoms free of charge without questioning her or notifying her parents. Knowing her parents would disapprove of her decision, Denise did not feel comfortable discussing it with them. She felt that she was old enough and mature enough to make her own decision about becoming sexually active. And she knew she wanted to use protection. Denise appreciated that her school treated her like an adult and made it easy for her to be sexually responsible.

Distributing condoms in schools appears to increase condom use. A George Washington University study compared differences in condom use among 4,166 sexually active Massachusetts

Parental Consent Laws

Americans have mixed feeling about parental consent laws. Parental consent policy on health issues involving minors varies from state to state and is often quite inconsistent. Most states require parental consent for the dispersion of medication and/or medical, dental, or hospital treatment of minors. But exceptions are common for minors seeking treatment involving sexual activity, mental health, or substance abuse. For example, all fifty states and the District of Columbia allow doctors to confidentially treat minors with a sexually transmitted infection.

In other cases parental consent requirements are less consistent. For instance, only two states and the District of Columbia explicitly allow minors confidential access to abortion. Twenty-one states require the consent of at least one parent; five states have no policy; and the remaining states have a mix of policies that involve some form of parental involvement.

Access to tattoos and body piercing also varies by state, with thirty-eight states prohibiting these procedures without parental consent. In some states tattooing a minor is illegal even with parental consent. Only three states allow minors confidential access to body art.

teenagers. Researchers found that students who attended schools that dispensed condoms were twice as likely to use a condom during their most recent sexual encounter as their counterparts who attended schools that did not dispense condoms. Distributing condoms in school clinics also may help reduce teen pregnancy. Patrick Welsh, a teacher at T.C. Williams High School in Alexandria, Virginia, where a school health clinic opened in 2010, can see the difference. "The most striking to me and other veteran teachers here on the front lines is that we have not been seeing as many girls making their way down the hallways seven or eight months pregnant,"[38] he says. Indeed, distributing condoms in schools appears to be so effective that the American Congress of Obstetricians and Gynecologists, the Institute of Medicine, the American Academy of Pediatrics (AAP), and the AMA recommend that condoms be made available to adolescents as part of school health programs.

Are Schools Overstepping Their Authority?

Nevertheless, many social conservatives do not support condom distribution in schools. They maintain that the policy weakens parents' fundamental right to remain free from governmental interference with their child rearing. When schools dispense condoms, they argue, schools are overstepping their authority. Legally, schools require parental consent to give students an aspirin, so why should they be allowed to give students condoms without parental consent? Doing so, they argue, makes students think having sex with a condom is safe, when condoms are not 100 percent effective in preventing pregnancy or all STIs. If condoms are not used correctly, or if they break during intercourse, results can include pregnancy or the transmission of an STI. Moreover, condoms only offer limited protection against two types of STIs—genital ulcer infections, like herpes, and HPV. According to the CDC, these infections can occur in genital areas not covered by a condom and can be transmitted through skin-to-skin contact with infected sores or skin. Condoms can only protect against transmission when the ulcers or infections are in genital areas that are protected by the condom. When schools distribute condoms, opponents of the policy say, young people get a false sense of security when, in reality, they are being put at risk. Randy Alcorn, an author, pastor, and the founder of Eternal Perspective Ministries in Sandy, Oregon, compares depending on a condom for protection to playing Russian roulette: "Wearing a condom does nothing more than remove a few bullets out of the gun's chamber. But when you're playing Russian roulette, eventually the one or two bullets left in the chamber are sure to kill you. Especially when taking out a few bullets makes you feel safer, so you can feel good about playing the game more often."[39]

In addition, critics say that distributing condoms in school encourages sexual activity in adolescents. However, this does not appear to be true. Studies that compared sexual activity and condom use among students in schools that distributed condoms with those in schools that did not found that the sexual activity rates of both groups were about the same. The primary difference, according to these studies, was in how often condoms were used; condom use was greater among the students with easy access to condoms than among other students. Similarly, in Canada and most of Europe, where confidential, easy access to condoms is the norm for teenagers, sexual activity rates are comparable and, in some cases, lower than those in the United States.

Alan J. Singer, an education professor at New York's Hofstra University, points out that just because young people have access to condoms does not mean they will have intercourse. He remembers his own experience in this way:

> When I was sixteen years old and a junior in high school, I got a condom somehow and began carrying it around in my wallet. . . . Sometimes in school, I'd show my condom to the guys so they would know that I was prepared. The condom went to summer camp with me that summer, hidden away with acne medicine and aftershave lotion. I never did get to use that condom. Its packaging deteriorated before I had the opportunity. Access to condoms does not mean teenagers are going to have sex. It means if they do have sex, it will more likely be safe sex.[40]

"Access to condoms does not mean teenagers are going to have sex. It means if they do have sex, it will more likely be safe sex."[40]

— Alan J. Singer, an education professor at Hofstra University.

Family Planning Clinics

When schools do not have health care clinics, school nurses may refer sexually active teens to a family planning clinic such as Planned Parenthood or the FPC. These clinics are funded by Title X and are therefore required under federal law to provide confidential reproductive health care to teens. Planned Parenthood runs more than 750 reproductive health clinics across the United

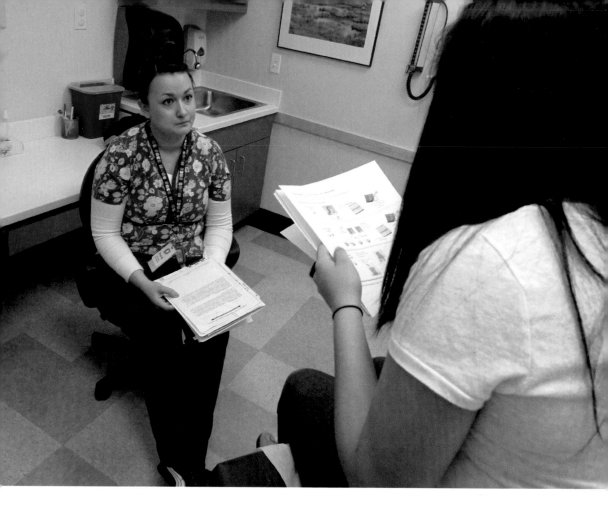

A Texas Planned Parenthood employee confers with a young patient. School nurses sometimes refer sexually active teens to family planning clinics such as Planned Parenthood for contraceptives and other services.

States that supply patients with contraceptives, birth control pills, breast cancer examinations, screening for cervical cancer, tests and treatments for STIs, pregnancy tests, and, in some cases, abortions. The clinics also perform vasectomies on males and test and treat males for STIs. Planned Parenthood serves about 3 million clients per year. Approximately 20 percent are teenagers. The organization estimates that its services help prevent 486,000 unintended pregnancies each year.

On a first visit to a clinic, patients are asked to fill out a medical history sheet. Then patients are taken to a private room to discuss birth control options with a health care professional. If the patient chooses birth control pills, she is given a prescription, which usually can be filled at the clinic. If she chooses an implanted birth control device, she is taken to an examining room where a health care professional implants the device. Before the patient leaves, a health care professional instructs her on how to use her chosen method of birth control. Most patients find the experience nonthreatening and say they were treated with dignity and respect.

Tampa Bay Times reporter Natalie Rella visited Planned Parenthood for the first time when she was sixteen. She felt a lot of pressure from her friends to be sexually active, but she was not sure if she was ready. She wanted to have protection just in case she decided to take that step. She did not feel comfortable talking to her parents, and she did not want to go to her family physician because she knew he would contact her parents. So she went to a local Planned Parenthood clinic. "As soon as I walked through the door, I felt like I was in a place that was safe and judgment-free," she recalls.

> After I signed in, I was shown to a private room to talk with a health educator. She gave me the birth control I wanted. But she also gave me the information I needed to make a responsible decision about when I would be ready to have sex. Based upon my conversation with her, I decided that I was not ready. I chose to wait. . . . I credit Planned Parenthood for giving me the tools—both education and birth control—I needed to make responsible decisions about my sexual health.[41]

The FPC provides similar services in twenty-one clinics in the United States. Some states, cities, hospitals, and private groups also run reproductive health clinics that provide confidential services to teenagers at no or low cost. These types of family planning clinics are found in all states and most large cities. According to a 2011 study by the Guttmacher Institute, more than eight thousand clinics throughout the country provide free or low-cost contraceptive services to teen and adult females.

Emergency Contraceptives

One of the most controversial forms of birth control that reproductive health clinics distribute is an emergency contraceptive pill commonly known as Plan B or the morning-after pill. The

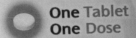

NDC 51285-942-88

Rx only for women younger than age 17

Plan B One-Step®

(levonorgestrel) tablet, 1.5 mg
Emergency Contraceptive

Reduces the chance of pregnancy after unprotected sex (if a regular birth control method fails or after sex without birth control)

Not for regular birth control.

One Tablet
One Dose

- Take as soon as possible within 72 hours (3 days) after unprotected sex. The sooner you take it, the better Plan B One-Step® will work.

1 Tablet
Levonorgestrel 1.5mg

Taken within seventy-two hours of unprotected sexual intercourse, the emergency contraceptive Plan B disrupts ovulation and thereby prevents pregnancy. Although previously available only by prescription for women under age seventeen, as of 2013 women of any age may buy this type of emergency contraceptive without a prescription.

morning-after pill consists of high doses of one or more female hormones. When these hormones are taken in a concentrated dose within seventy-two hours after unprotected intercourse, they prevent pregnancy 89 percent of the time. The pill works by disrupting ovulation, or the release of a fertilized egg. It is also possible, but not proven, that the pill may prevent a fertilized egg from being implanted on the uterine wall. If a fertilized egg has already implanted on the uterine wall, the pill is ineffective. The American medical community widely agrees that pregnancy begins upon successful implantation. The pill is most effective if it is taken within twelve to twenty-four hours of sexual activity.

Up until 2006 emergency contraceptives were available by prescription only. That year, however, the US Food and Drug Administration ruled that anyone age eighteen and older could purchase the drug without a prescription, much like condoms. In 2009 access was extended to individuals seventeen and older.

It was further extended to individuals fifteen or older in 2013. That same year a federal judge lifted the age ban entirely, allowing females of any age to confidentially buy emergency contraception without a prescription.

The ruling has caused heated debate. Many medical organizations support the ruling, including the AAP. Dr. Thomas McInerny, president of the AAP, explains: "While pediatricians recommend that teens delay sexual activity until they fully understand its consequences, we strongly encourage the use of contraception—including emergency contraception—to protect the health of our adolescent patients who are sexually active."[42]

Opponents have multiple concerns. Many conservative Christians believe that life begins with the union of a sperm and an egg. In their opinion, the emergency contraceptive is an abortion-producing pill, something to which they are morally opposed. They also are concerned that taking the pill, especially if it is used repeatedly, may cause health issues for young teens. "This drug has not been studied for safety for girls 16 and under," says Dr. Donna Harrison, director of the American Association of Pro-life Obstetricians and Gynecologists. "We have no studies on the long-term effects of unlimited and unsupervised ingestion of hormones. . . . [Lifting the age ban] defies sense."[43]

"We strongly encourage the use of contraception—including emergency contraception—to protect the health of our adolescent patients who are sexually active."[42]

— Dr. Thomas McInerny, president of the AAP.

Making Safe Choices

Despite groups that oppose giving teens access to contraceptives, today's young people have greater access to birth control than ever before, with laws in place that help protect their privacy. But it is still up to each teenager to make safe choices. As teenaged Sammy insists, "If you are going to have sex, think it through and be smart. Go to your local drug store and buy a pack of condoms or go on the pill (or other form of birth control) and [if] you cannot bring yourself to do that then you are clearly not ready for sex."[44]

Facts

- According to the Guttmacher Institute, a sexually active female who does not use contraceptives has an 85 percent chance of becoming pregnant within a year.

- The Guttmacher Institute reports that some teens face violence from their parents as a result of informing them that they are seeking birth control.

- Planned Parenthood relates that less than 1 percent of women who take a birth control pill every day become pregnant.

- According to a 2012 NCPTUP poll, eight out of ten parents who responded to the poll said they hoped their children would talk to them if they were sexually active so they could ensure that their children had access to birth control.

- According to the Guttmacher Institute, teens who use contraceptives during their first sexual experience are more likely to continue using contraceptives throughout their lives.

How Does the Media Influence Teen Pregnancy?

S mart phones, computers, tablets, televisions, gaming devices, and MP3 players are an essential part of modern life, especially for teenagers. According to a 2010 survey by the Kaiser Family Foundation, American teens spend approximately seven and a half hours a day consuming media, about as much time as adults spend working. That number rises to more than ten hours when multitasking is factored in.

The media provides young people with entertainment, information, social contacts, and role models. Its influence on young people, their sexual activity, and teen pregnancy cannot be underestimated. As the NCPTUP explains, "The media shapes the social script for teens. . . . From the latest must have fashions to celebrity baby bumps to what is seen as normative behavior—the media helps paint the canvas of what is cool for teens."[45]

Reality Television

Maci Bookout became pregnant with her son, Bentley, at age sixteen. When her mother heard that MTV was casting for the reality show *16 and Pregnant*, she urged Maci to submit a casting tape.

In 2009 Maci became the first of four girls featured on the show, which followed the story of each girl dealing with the difficulties of being pregnant. After their babies were born, Maci and the other girls were featured on *Teen Mom*, a sequel to *16 and Pregnant* that documented the girls' lives as parents. *Teen Mom* became one of the most highly rated shows on MTV, and Maci and the other girls became celebrities. They appeared on talk shows and on the covers of tabloids and magazines like *People*, *OK!*, and *Us*.

The young mothers' celebrity status earned them a large fan base and made them role models for viewers. Critics of the show say that *Teen Mom* glamorizes teen pregnancy and sends teens the message that if they become pregnant, they might get on the show and become rich and famous. In fact, when three friends of Jenelle Evans, a teen mother featured on *Teen Mom 2* (a sequel to *Teen Mom*) became pregnant, there was speculation on the Internet that the girls purposefully became pregnant in hopes of following in Jenelle's footsteps. According to teen author Gaby Rodriguez, "Lots of us feel invisible in our regular lives. When kids don't feel like they stand out for any reason, sometimes they look for ways to get noticed. So the real danger of these shows is that teens who are easily influenced may say, 'If I get pregnant, I could go on a show like that and get famous. People would pay attention to me.'"[46]

Lauren Dolgen, the creator of *16 and Pregnant* and *Teen Mom*, insists that glamorizing teen pregnancy is not her intent. Her aim is to prevent teen pregnancy by educating viewers to the hardships of teen pregnancy and parenthood. "This [teen pregnancy] is an epidemic, but it's a preventable epidemic,"[47] she says.

The shows seem to be having the desired effect. A 2011 survey by the NCPTUP found that 80 percent of the teens who watched *Teen Mom* and responded to the survey said the program showed them the consequences and difficulties of teen pregnancy and strengthened their desire to avoid an early pregnancy. Sarah Brown, the chief executive officer of the NCPTUP, says the shows are excellent teaching tools:

"From the latest must have fashions to celebrity baby bumps to what is seen as normative behavior—the media helps paint the canvas of what is cool for teens."[45]

— National Campaign to Prevent Teen and Unplanned Pregnancy.

Jenelle Evans, one of the teen moms featured on MTV's Teen Mom 2, walks with her son. Critics say shows such as this one glamorize teen pregnancy and may even encourage teens to seek celebrity by getting pregnant.

This generation of young people, teens, have grown up on reality shows. They really get this idea that this is somebody who's not an actor, they're telling the truth, they're followed over time. And I think it packs a reality to them that just cannot be re-created in a classroom. And so we often call these shows sort of sex-ed in the 21st century. And it's in a medium that young people like. It's not a lecture with a blackboard. It's on television, online, in a media environment that teens live in.[48]

Sending Mixed Messages

While the intent of *16 and Pregnant* and *Teen Mom* might be to reduce teen pregnancy by showing viewers the hardships teen pregnancy and parenting entail, other television shows send a very different message. They present unprotected, early casual sex as normal, risk free, and glamorous while portraying abstinence as abnormal. Television shows aimed at teens like *Glee*, *Vampire Diaries,* and *Gossip Girl* have featured sexually explicit scenes. More often than not, it is the popular kids—the kids whom viewers emulate—who are sexually active. Other sexually explicit network television shows geared toward adults, like *The Bachelor*, *New Girl,* and *Two Broke Girls*, as well as cable programs like *Girls* and *True Blood*, also draw a wide teen audience. But even crime dramas, cartoons, talk shows, soap operas, and news programs can be sexually provocative. According to the Media Project, a Los Angeles–based media group associated with the adolescent reproductive health organization Advocates for Youth, two out of every three television shows contain sexual content. Yet only about 10 percent of shows with sexual content include any reference to pregnancy or contraception.

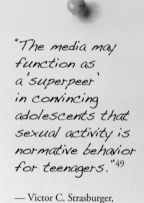

"The media may function as a 'superpeer' in convincing adolescents that sexual activity is normative behavior for teenagers."[49]

— Victor C. Strasburger, pediatrician.

Being bombarded with seemingly carefree sexual activity on television has a powerful influence on young people. A Rand Corporation study found that teens are twice as likely to have sex or engage in sexual acts if they see similar sexual behavior on television or in movies. In an APA article, pediatrician and lead author Victor C. Strasburger explains: "American media make sex seem like a harmless sport in which everyone engages, and results of considerable research have indicated that the media can have a major effect on young people's attitudes and behaviors. In fact, the media may function as a 'superpeer' in convincing adolescents that sexual activity is normative behavior for teenagers."[49]

Other studies indicate that viewing sexual content on television and in movies increases the likelihood that young people will initiate first sex at a younger age than those whose viewing is restricted. A University of North Carolina study found that young teens exposed to television programs with high sexual content were more likely to have sex by age sixteen than their peers whose viewing was limited. Similarly, a 2012 Dartmouth University study on movie viewing found that young teens who are exposed to movies with the most sexual content are more likely to lose their virginity at a younger age than their peers who do not view these movies. As David Bickham, the coauthor of a similar Boston Children's Hospital study, explains, "Children have neither the life experience nor the brain development to fully differentiate between a reality they are moving toward and a fiction meant solely to entertain. Children learn from media, and when they watch media with sexual references and innuendos, our research suggests they are more likely to engage in sexual activity earlier in life."[50]

> "Children learn from media, and when they watch media with sexual references and innuendos, our research suggests they are more likely to engage in sexual activity earlier in life."[50]
>
> — David Bickham, staff scientist at the Center on Media and Child Health at Boston Children's Hospital.

Sexual Messages in Music Lyrics and Videos

Music lyrics, music videos, and performances by popular singers have become increasingly sexually explicit and, like television shows and movies, appear to influence teen sexual attitudes and behavior. Popular performers like Nicki Minaj, Nelly, Eminem, Bruno Mars, Ludacris, Ciara, Chris Brown, Usher, Rihanna, and Christina Aguilera, among others, have recorded songs with sexually provocative lyrics and have appeared in sexually suggestive live performances and music videos. Many of these songs depict females as sexual objects, portray males as sexual aggressors, and promote an unhealthy sexual message.

A University of Pittsburgh study found that one-third of popular music contains references to sexual intercourse, with references being even more prevalent in rap, hip-hop, and heavy metal music. Adolescents spend about two and a half hours a day listening to music. The University of Pittsburgh study suggests that teens who listen to a cross section of popular music are exposed to about forty-eight minutes a day of sexually explicit music and thirty-two minutes a day of sexually degrading music. The impact music has on teens cannot be underestimated. "Music," according to the NCPTUP, "is often the medium that defines and may help shape young people's romantic ideals and expectations."[51]

Being exposed to sexually explicit music appears to negatively affect young people in a number of ways. For instance, a Rand Corporation study found that teens who listen to sexually explicit music are twice as likely to be sexually active as teens who listen to less sexually charged music. Moreover, according to a 2011 Brigham Young University study, listening to sexual lyrics influences teen relationships and the way they view themselves and each other. The study found that exposure to sexually explicit music leads young men to view females as sexual objects and young women to value themselves based on their appearance and sexuality. These beliefs may influence young people to lower their inhibitions and experiment sexually. According to the NCPTUP, compared to their peers, teens who listen to sexually degrading music are more likely to have sexual intercourse and multiple sexual partners and are less likely to use contraception. As Brigham Young University researchers explain, "Popular music can teach young men to be sexually aggressive and treat women as objects while often teaching young women that their value to society is to provide sexual pleasure for others. It is essential for society that sex education providers are aware of these issues and their impact on adolescent sexual behavior."[52]

> "Music is often the medium that defines and may help shape young people's romantic ideals and expectations."[51]
>
> — National Campaign to Prevent Teen and Unplanned Pregnancy.

Opportunities on the Internet

The Internet also plays an important part in the lives of teens. In fact, it is their primary media choice. Teenagers spend more time online than with any other media. According to a 2012 Yahoo! study, young people ages thirteen to twenty-four spend 16.7 hours a week online, excluding e-mail. They spend some of this time seeking information about issues affecting their lives, including information about sex. A 2012 Guttmacher Institute survey found that 55 percent of seventh to twelfth graders who responded to the survey said that they have looked up health information online. It is not uncommon for teens to say that they learned more about sexual

Rihanna (pictured in concert in 2013) is just one of many popular performers whose songs have sexually explicit lyrics and who appear in sexually suggestive videos and live performances. Some studies show that sexually charged music influences sexual activity among teens.

health from the Internet than from sex education classes in school. Take Nicole, a teenager who had unplanned, unprotected sex with her boyfriend, then panicked at the thought that she might become pregnant. Not knowing what to do, she went online seeking information. She learned about emergency contraception in her online search. As a result, she visited a local reproductive clinic, which she also located online, and was given the pill she needed.

Although not all websites provide accurate information about sexual health, many do. And many teens depend on the Internet for information about sexuality. Organizations like the NCPTUP,

Planned Parenthood, the Guttmacher Institute, the CDC, the Adolescent Pregnancy Prevention Campaign of North Carolina (APPCNC), the American Sexual Health Association, and many state health departments are reliable online sources of sexual health information. Some also answer questions online, have text-messaging hotlines, and offer live chats, forums, and cell phone apps.

Exposure to Internet Pornography

Other sexual content on the Internet is not as helpful. In fact, it can have a harmful impact on teens. The Internet gives young people access to pornography. Some teens actively seek it out, but others are exposed to it inadvertently while searching for other topics. A 2008 joint study by the Pennsylvania State University and the University of New Hampshire found that 93 percent of boys and 62 percent of girls are exposed to Internet pornography before they reach the age of eighteen. According to Patricia Greenfield, a psychology professor at the University of California, Los Angeles (UCLA), and the director of UCLA's Children's Digital Media Center, "Childhood used to be a time of relative innocence . . . but with today's all-pervasive sexualized media environment, that is no longer the case. By late childhood, it has become very difficult to avoid highly sexualized material that is intended for an adult audience."[53]

Sex in pornography is rarely portrayed in terms of relationships or emotions. It is usually presented as purely physical, unplanned, and sometimes violent, bizarre, or degrading. Contraception, pregnancy, and STIs are seldom mentioned. Studies have shown that teens who are regularly exposed to pornography are more likely to have casual sex than teens who are not regularly exposed to it. Moreover, teenage boys who regularly view pornography tend to view females as sex objects. Females who regularly view pornography often measure their self-worth in terms of their sexuality. In the publication *Managing the Media Monster: The Influence of the Media (from Television to Text Messages) on Teen Sexual Behavior and Attitudes*, the NCPTUP explains that in pornography,

> sex is presented as a commodity. If young peoples' initial explorations of sex happen in the context of the sex-

ual marketplace rather than learning about connecting and developing relationships with others, how are they to develop healthy concepts of romance, relationships, and responsibilities around sex? Seen in this context, the phenomenon of "friends with benefits," in which young people with no romantic relationship have sex with each other out of boredom or a need for "something to do," is hardly surprising.[54]

The National Day to Prevent Teen Pregnancy

Since 2001 the National Day to Prevent Teen Pregnancy has been observed on May 1. Organized by the NCPTUP, the National Day is supported by more than two hundred partnering organizations, including media outlets, faith-based groups, businesses, educational institutions, health care agencies, and youth groups. These groups help promote the National Day to their members, clients, and audiences.

The purpose of the day is to focus attention on the importance of avoiding early pregnancy and parenthood and to help teens think carefully about relationships, sexual activity, contraception, pregnancy, and parenthood. On the National Day, and throughout the month of May, teens are encouraged to participate in an online quiz at the website StayTeen.org. Through a series of interactive scenarios, the quiz challenges participants to think about what they might do in different situations involving romance, relationships, and sex. More than seven hundred thousand teens participate in the quiz annually. Eighty-five percent of the participants say that taking the quiz made them think about what they might do in such situations, and 58 percent say the quiz taught them something new about the consequences of sex.

The Power of Social Media

The Internet also gives teens access to social media. A 2013 Pew Foundation study found that eight out of ten online teens use some kind of social media. Of these teens, 81 percent use Facebook, 24 percent use Twitter, and many use both. Seventy-five percent of teenage social media users visit the sites at least once a day, and 48 percent visit several times a day. As Nicole Chisolm, a teen health activist and blogger, relates, "Facebook, Twitter, YouTube—we're there. I don't think I can name five friends who do not have a Facebook or Twitter page. And I definitely can't think of anyone who doesn't utilize YouTube."[55]

As with the Internet, social media can be both a positive and negative force in reducing teen pregnancy. Many health organizations have established a social media presence in an effort to connect with teenagers and prevent teen pregnancy. Being on social media allows organizations to reach a large audience and helps individuals to connect with each other in an ever-widening network. For example, the CDC has a link for social media and teen pregnancy on its website. Visitors can post cut-and-paste messages aimed at reducing teen pregnancy on their personal Facebook pages. In turn, visitors to these individuals' personal Facebook pages who like the messages can add them to their own page. Friends of their friends can do the same, and so on. Since the average Facebook user has 135 friends, the number of posts keeps multiplying. Each new post reaches a new and continually expanding network of people.

On the other hand, the freedom social media gives teens can lead to trouble. Many teens post sexual messages and provocative pictures of themselves on their Facebook pages. Some teenagers post suggestive videos of themselves on YouTube. Although many young people say such actions are all in fun, this type of activity can lower the sexual inhibitions of posters and viewers, thereby encouraging teens to be more sexually active. A 2008 survey by the blog *CosmoGirl* found that, of the teens answering the survey, 38 percent said that exchanging sexually suggestive pictures on social media makes having sex more likely. Moreover, such postings may attract the attention of sexual predators.

Public Service Announcements

Other media sources, like public service announcements (PSAs), do not send mixed messages. PSAs utilize the media to raise awareness of important social issues such as teen pregnancy. Traditionally, PSAs have appeared on billboards, in ads on mass transit, and in print media. They are also aired on television, radio, and in

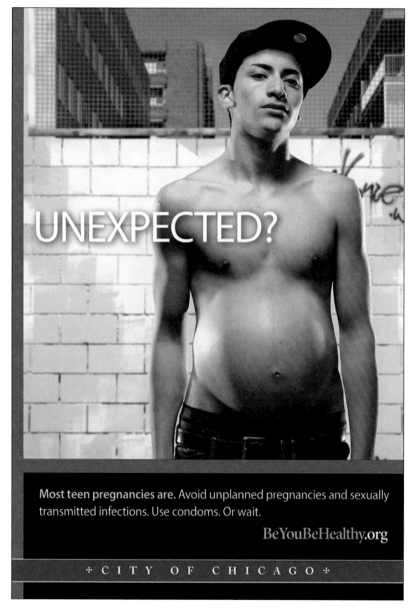

UNEXPECTED?

Most teen pregnancies are. Avoid unplanned pregnancies and sexually transmitted infections. Use condoms. Or wait.

BeYouBeHealthy.org

✦ C I T Y   O F   C H I C A G O ✦

An eye-catching poster showing a boy with a pregnant belly appears in Chicago, Illinois. The posters are aimed at getting people to think about teen pregnancies and teen births. This poster urges youths to use condoms—or wait until they are older to have sex.

movie theaters. And, in an effort to attract the attention of young people, they are now posted on YouTube.

Many teen pregnancy prevention PSAs posted on YouTube were made by teenagers for a teenage audience. Some of these videos were made in response to school projects or as entries to contests run by health organizations such as the NCPTUP, the Massachusetts Alliance on Teen Pregnancy, or the APPCNC, among others. These PSAs appear to have a positive effect on the teens who create them as well as on the target audience. Creating these videos raises the maker's awareness about the problem, which should make the teen more cautious in his or her sexual behavior. And, because these videos are created by their peers, young viewers can relate to their message. Most of these PSAs receive thousands of hits.

Other PSAs aimed at reducing teen pregnancy try to catch the attention of teens in creative and quirky ways. For instance, in 2013 the Chicago Department of Public Health posted ads on mass transit featuring doctored images of teenage boys made to look pregnant. The word *unexpected* was displayed prominently on the ad. Below the picture, a caption explained that most teen pregnancies are unexpected and advised teens to use condoms or wait to have sex. "We wanted to create an ad campaign that would cut through the clutter and get people thinking about teen pregnancy and teen births, and how it can affect more than just teen girls,"[56] Brian Richardson, a spokesperson for the Chicago Department of Public Health, explains.

Teen pregnancy prevention PSAs were also posted in mass transit throughout New York City in 2013. These ads, which featured an interactive texting component and video, caused a lot of controversy. Known as the "Think Being a Teen Parent Won't Cost You?" campaign, the PSAs used hard-hitting facts about the costs and negative consequences of teen parenting to send an anti–teen pregnancy message. The ads feature the faces of crying toddlers and the following captions: "I'm twice as likely not to finish high school because you had me as a teen"; "Honestly mom, chances are he won't stay with you. What happens to me?"; "Dad, you'll be paying support for me for the next 20 years"; "Got a good job? I cost thousands of dollars each year"; and "If you finish high

Preventing Teen Pregnancy with Text Messages

The nonprofit organization DoSomething.org works with young people for social change on a wide range of issues. One of its campaigns uses cell phones to prevent teen pregnancy. The organization challenges teens to be virtual parents for a day. Teens sign up by submitting their phone number and those of five friends. The teen and his or her friends then receive ten text messages from a virtual baby during a twenty-four-hour period. The messages emphasize the difficulties of teen parenting. Here is an example of a message: "What's that smell? Oh . . . it's me. We've got a situation downtown. I know you're busy, but I need to be changed ASAP. Answer the call of doodie and freshen me up!" DoSomething.org hopes that the experience will make participants of both genders realize how much their lives would change if they were parents and encourage them to think more carefully about their sexual behavior.

Quoted in Kate, "Use Your Cell Phone to Prevent Teen Pregnancies," Heart of Gold, May 21, 2012. www.heartofgoldgirls.com.

school, get a good job and get married before having children, you have a 98% chance of not living in poverty."[57]

Critics of the ads worry about the potential stigma they might bring to teen parents. The ads, critics say, are mean-spirited, using shame and guilt to get their point across. Supporters counter that making teens aware of the harsh reality of teen pregnancy is the best way to solve the problem. According to New York City mayor Michael Bloomberg:

> This campaign makes very clear to young people that there's a lot at stake when it comes to deciding to raise a child. We've already seen important progress in our effort to help

more teens delay pregnancy. . . . We aim to build on our success by asking teens to take an honest look at some of the realities of parenthood they may not have considered. By focusing on responsibility and the importance of education, employment, and family in providing children with the emotional and financial support they need, we'll let thousands of young New Yorkers know that waiting to become a parent could be the best decision they ever make.[58]

The Answer Is Ambiguous

It is clear that the media has a big impact on teens. It can be a tool for entertainment as well as education. Yet whether the media has a responsibility to address social issues like teen pregnancy remains ambiguous. The media cannot be blamed for any individual's actions, whether good or bad. But, knowing the tremendous influence the media has on young people, many organizations are using it in hopes of reducing teen pregnancy.

Facts

- According to a 2012 NCPTUP poll, 73 percent of teens say that what they see in the media about sex can be a good start to a discussion with adults about sex.

- According to the Kaiser Family Foundation, the number of sexual images on television has nearly doubled since 1998.

- The American Psychological Association estimates that teenagers are exposed to a total of fourteen thousand sexual references and sexual innuendos per year on television.

- According to the NCPTUP, teens tend to overestimate the sexual activity of their peers. One source of this misconception is the media.

What Else Can Be Done to Reduce Teen Pregnancy?

Although the teen pregnancy rate is currently at a nearly forty-year low, because of the impact teen pregnancy has on individuals and society there is a general consensus that more needs to be done. Sex education, access to contraceptives, and positive media efforts help, but none of these strategies is a perfect solution. In an effort to do more, a number of organizations are taking a broader approach. Some are focusing on societal factors that make teens vulnerable to risky behavior. Others are centering their attention on reducing repeat pregnancies in teen mothers. Some are looking at other countries for guidance, and others are seeking guidance from teens themselves.

Teens at Risk

Gaby Rodriguez is a young woman who faked her own pregnancy for a school research project and then wrote a book about her experience. Although she is a serious person who avoids risky behavior, when she announced that she was pregnant many people who knew her were not surprised. After all, she is the daughter of a teen mother, she is Hispanic, and she is socioeconomically disadvantaged—three factors that put her at risk of teen pregnancy.

Daughters of teen mothers are three times more likely to become teen mothers themselves than daughters of women who wait to have children. Gaby's mother became pregnant with her first child when she was fourteen. The cycle had already repeated itself in Gaby's family. Her four siblings had all been pregnant or caused a pregnancy as teens. "I'd been fighting the stereotypes myself," she explains. "Because of my family's history, as soon as I started dating people would say, 'You're going to get pregnant in high school just like Jessica [her sister].'"[59] Being Hispanic and socioeconomically disadvantaged added to Gaby's risk. According to the CDC, Hispanics, followed by African Americans, have the highest rates of teen pregnancy in the United States. In 2011 Hispanic teen birthrates were 49.4 per 1,000 births, compared to 47.4 per 1,000 for African Americans and 21.8 per 1,000 for non-Hispanic whites.

Rates also are high among socioeconomically disadvantaged teens of all ethnicities. Although there is no clear explanation for this, a number of studies indicate it is common for socioeconomically disadvantaged teens to feel hopeless about the future, which makes them more prone to engage in risky behavior like having unprotected sex. Other individual, social, and family factors that put girls at risk of teen pregnancy include having low self-esteem, a lack of parental supervision, an absent father, living in a group home or foster care, poor school performance, being the victim of sexual abuse, dating at an early age, dating older partners, and having friends who are sexually active.

Empowering Teens

Although many of these risk factors cannot be changed, by giving teens more hope for the future, help in school, and a support network, a number of innovative programs are making strides in reducing teen pregnancy. As author Lisa Covitch explains, "Young people are more likely to avoid teen pregnancy when they believe in a positive future for themselves. Schools and communities must

> "Schools and communities must formulate powerful strategies for those young people who live on the margins, who are unsuccessful in school, who do not have nurturing families, and who live in disadvantaged communities."[60]
>
> — Lisa Covitch, author of *The Epidemic of Teen Pregnancy: An American Tragedy*, and field care manager for Community Behavioral Health Network of Pennsylvania.

the person working with her is an important factor in preventing repeat teen pregnancies.

One Baltimore, Maryland, home-based program cultivates this relationship by pairing teen mothers with college-educated single mothers who act as big sisters to the younger women. The older women give the young mothers lessons in decision making, goal setting, personal values, contraceptive use, and family planning as well as being caring, nonjudgmental mentors. The program seems to help. The teen mothers who received the Baltimore intervention were two and a half times less likely to have a second birth within two years of the birth of their first child than young mothers in a control group.

What Do Teens Think?

Other organizations are taking a different approach. They are polling teens to determine what they think about sexuality, pregnancy, and sex education. The goal of these polls is to make sure established and new programs meet teens' needs. Birth control—how it works, how to use it, and where to get it—is one thing that seems to be on the minds of many young people. In a 2012 Planned Parenthood nationwide survey, 75 percent of teen respondents said they needed more information about birth control. In a 2012 survey by the NCPTUP, 72 percent of survey participants said they knew little or nothing about birth control pills, and 47 percent said they knew little or nothing about condoms and how to use them. As teenage Kristin wrote in an essay for a contest sponsored by A Woman's Choice Clinic in Yakima, Washington, "People need to face the fact that most teens are sexually active. . . . The best options that we have are to make birth control more accessible, available, and accepted."[64]

Being able to talk about sex is also on teens' minds. The NCPTUP survey found that teens say their parents are the most influential people in their lives when it comes to making decisions about sex. Eighty-seven percent of the teens responding to the survey said it would be easier for them to delay sexual activity and avoid teen pregnancy if they and their parents could have open conversations about sex. Indeed, studies have shown that adolescents who feel close to and supported by their parents are more likely to delay sexual intercourse, consistently use contraceptives if they are sexually active, and have fewer sexual partners than teens who have poor relationships with their parents. According to Brynn, a California teen:

> In terms of educating me for sex, I think that they [parents] should play a really big role. Sex is something that we're inundated with every day, images everywhere, yet it's still kind of a taboo subject. . . . I've never really had my

Helping Teen Parents Finish High School

Many high schools throughout the United States have implemented special programs to help parenting teens graduate. One of the most popular is the nationwide Teen Outreach Program. By providing teen parents with support and hope for the future, these programs may help prevent teen parents from having a repeat teen pregnancy. Each program is different. Most have a number of components. One of the most vital is a school-based day-care center staffed by trained workers. Teen parents drop their children off at the day-care center at the start of the day and pick them up after school. Teen parents are encouraged to drop in to the center during the day, and nursing mothers have the time they need to nurse factored into their class schedule. In many schools, parenting teens are required to work in the day-care center for one class period a day, for which they receive class credit.

Parenting classes are part of most programs. Some programs also offer contraceptive and health care services and connect teens with support services. Many programs also offer teen parents special tutoring and extra excused absences.

parents come in and be like, "We need to talk" and sit down with me. We have so many questions and we're just waiting for someone to talk to us, and I think parents need to do that a lot more than they are.[65]

Not only do teens want their parents to have more open conversations about sex with them, but they also want the adults in their lives to be more realistic about teen sexuality. As teenage Crissa wrote in her A Woman's Choice Clinic essay, "If parents, step parents, grandparents, and society as a whole or even as a half, accepted teenage sex they would have a better chance at communication between parents and children and lowering the teenage pregnancy rate."[66]

Getting Parents Involved

Despite the important role parents play in teen decision making, many parents say they are uncomfortable talking to their children about sex. Melissa Havard, a California public health specialist, explains: "It's often one of the most feared moments for parents—ever. . . . It seems like we can talk to our children about so many things. . . . Yet, when it comes to sex, our throat tightens up, we get all red in the face, and we usually say something along the lines of: 'Mary, you're not having sex, are you? Ok, good! Phew.'"[67]

A 2011 Planned Parenthood survey, which polled parents about their attitudes toward talking to their children about sex, found that 57 percent of the parents who responded to the survey said they feel only somewhat comfortable or uncomfortable about talking to their children about sex. The survey also found that even among parents who feel comfortable talking to their children about sex, many are ill at ease about talking about birth control and how to say no to sexual pressure. Another problem is that many parents wait too long to broach sexual topics with their children. By the time they do, their children may already be sexually active. But even delayed sexual discussions have an impact on adolescents. Indeed, experts, health care professionals, and teens all agree that sex education should begin at home. Havard agrees:

Honest discussions at early ages can lead to honest communication throughout childhood and through the tumultuous teen years, where often crucial decisions are made. Instead of cutting our children off, making them feel embarrassed, shaming, or threatening . . . we should calmly, openly, and when possible, with humor, encourage a discussion. When your kids trust you about discussions of sex, they will trust you about so many other aspects of their lives.[68]

In an effort to harness the influence parents have on teens' sexual decision making, a number of programs are working with parents to help them become more comfortable talking to their children about sex. In order to reach as many people as possible, programs are being offered in the places parents are most likely to be found. One program, known as Plain Talk, uses counselors known as "walkers and talkers" who go out into communities to talk to parents about communicating with teens about sex. One component of the program is home health parties. Counselors invite their neighbors into their homes for an informal get-together, during which they share information about reproductive health and practice communication skills. Getting together with neighbors and friends with shared concerns makes what could be a stressful experience less so.

The CDC takes another program, known as Talking Parents, Healthy Teens, to worksites. Talking Parents, Healthy Teens consists of eight one-hour sessions designed to help parents improve their communication skills about sex. Bringing the program to worksites makes it easy for busy parents to attend. A free lunch is served during the sessions, which is an added incentive for attending. Other programs entice parents to attend meetings by offering inducements like raffles, door prizes, and snacks. A program run by the Carrera program provides a hot meal, transportation, and babysitting service at every session. Other programs offer stipends to parents for completing a program assessment after attending all the sessions. Most participants who complete these programs say they feel more at ease about talking

"When your kids trust you about discussions of sex, they will trust you about so many other aspects of their lives."[68]

— Melissa Havard, a public health specialist.

Communication between parents and children about sex can strongly influence the choices teens make. Many experts say frank discussions about sex can help reduce the number of teen pregnancies.

with their children about sex. After the training, some parents hold discussions with their children about sex for the very first time.

Looking at Other Nations

Since teen pregnancy rates are lower in other industrialized countries, some organizations are looking at these nations for guidance. Countries with low teen pregnancy rates appear to have many things in common. One commonality is their view of teen sexuality. In the United States teen sexuality is often viewed as risky and shameful. In most of western Europe, where teen pregnancy rates are low, teen sexuality is viewed as a natural part of human development. As Pierre-Andre Michaud, chief of adolescent health at the University of Lausanne Hospital in Switzerland, explains, "In many European countries—Switzerland in particular—sexual intercourse, at least from the age of 15 or 16 years, is considered acceptable and even part of normative adolescent behavior."[69]

At the same time, western European teens are expected to be sexually responsible. In most western European countries contraceptives are easily accessible for people of all ages and are usually free for teens. Young people are taught to use them, and most do. Contraceptive education begins at an early age in schools, homes, and through widespread public education campaigns on the Internet, billboards, television, and radio and in movie theaters and health care facilities. The media is an active partner in these campaigns, which are straightforward and focus on both safety and pleasure. For example, a public service announcement on Dutch television instructs the public on how to unroll and put on a condom.

This strategy appears to be working. Teens in Europe use contraceptives much more consistently than American teens. The greatest difference is in the use of birth control pills among females. Compared to American young women, German teens are five times as likely to use birth control pills, and the Dutch are almost six times as likely. According to a report about teen pregnancy prevention programs in Europe by Advocates for Youth, "Young people believe it is 'stupid and irresponsible' to have sex without protection. Youth rely on the maxim 'safe sex or no sex.'"[70]

In western Europe, preventing teen pregnancy is seen as a public health issue in which politics and/or religion play no part. Most parents address the issue through open discussions about sex with their children. Schools do their part through comprehensive, age-appropriate sex education, which often begins as early

> "In many European countries—Switzerland in particular—sexual intercourse, at least from the age of 15 or 16 years, is considered acceptable and even part of normative adolescent behavior."[69]
>
> — Pierre-Andre Michaud, chief of adolescent health at the University of Lausanne Hospital, Switzerland.

as preschool. Unlike in many American schools, the focus is on preventing pregnancy rather than on abstinence, and condom use is encouraged. "My feeling is that it is impossible to have a double message toward young people," Michaud explains. "You can't say at the same time, 'Be abstinent, it's the only fair, good way, to escape from having HIV' . . . and at the same time say, 'Look, if you ever happen to have sex, then please do that and that and that.' You probably have to choose the message."[71]

Progress Is Being Made

Using these strategies as a guide, many American school districts are implementing comprehensive sex education starting in kindergarten. Reproductive health care advocates are putting pressure on the government to make contraceptives more accessible to young people. Other groups are working to open discussion channels between parents and teens. However, the sexual openness of many European countries and the acceptance that sexual activity is a part of adolescent development is not likely to be embraced by social conservatives in the United States. Indeed, since the 1960s, when teen pregnancy became a source of societal concern, how to deal with it has been a source of controversy. Opposing views on politics, religion, morality, education, and economics all play a part. Clearly, there is no easy answer to preventing teen pregnancy.

Yet despite the controversy, declining teen pregnancy rates indicate that progress is being made. Although more must be done, getting parents and the media involved, addressing risk factors, and arming teens with the knowledge they need to make good decisions are steps in the right direction.

Facts

- According to a 2012 NCPTUP survey, 38 percent of teen respondents said their parents most influence their sexual decisions, compared to 22 percent who cite their peers.

- Also in a 2012 NCPTUP survey, 71 percent of adults responding to the survey support federal funding for programs that have been proven to change teen sexual activity.

- Based on data from the National Vital Statistics System and two national surveys, the CDC reports that 76 percent of female teenagers surveyed and 62 percent of male teenagers surveyed have spoken to their parents about either abstinence or birth control.

- The CDC reports that among sexually active teens surveyed, 20 percent of females and 31 percent of males have never spoken with their parents about birth control or saying no to sex.

- Advocates for Youth reports that American teens have sex at the same rate as European teens, but European teens have a much lower pregnancy rate.

Source Notes

Introduction: Why Is Teen Pregnancy a Problem?

1. Quoted in Candies Foundation, "Diary of a Teen Mom, Interview with Taylor Yoxheimer, 18." www.candiesfoundation.org.
2. Erika Christakis, "The Good News in Teen Births Isn't Good Enough," *Time*, May 8, 2012. http://ideas.time.com.
3. Quoted in Lindsey Anderson, "Teen Moms Share Challenges, Triumphs," *Las Cruces (NM) Sun News*, May 14, 2013, p. 1A.
4. Annie E. Casey Foundation, "Teen Pregnancy at a Record Low in the United States," September 2006. www.aecf.org.

Chapter One: What Are the Origins of Concerns About Teen Pregnancy?

5. Quoted in Sabrina Zeigler, "Local Native Writes Book About Being Teen Mom in the 1960s," *Recorder Online*, March 24, 2011. www.recorderonline.com.
6. Frank F. Furstenberg Jr., "Bringing Back the Shotgun Wedding," *National Affairs*, Winter 1988, p. 121.
7. Quoted in Australian Broadcasting Company, "Time Frame Full Circle." www.abc.net.au.
8. Quoted in PBS, "Summer of Love." www.pbs.org.
9. Quoted in Frank F. Furstenberg, *Destinies of the Disadvantaged: The Politics of Teenage Childbearing*. New York: Russell Sage Foundation, 2007, p. 15.
10. Maris Vinovskis, "An 'Epidemic' of Adolescent Pregnancy? Some Historical Considerations," *Journal of Family History*, Summer 1981, p. 207. http://deepblue.lib.umich.edu.
11. Cynthia Dallard, "Reviving Interest in Policies and Programs to Help Teens Prevent Repeat Births," *The Guttmacher Report on Public Policy*, June 2000, Guttmacher Institute. www.guttmacher.org.
12. Quoted in McLaughlin Group, "Transcripts: The McLaughlin Group," May 26–27, 2007. www.mclaughlin.com.
13. Quoted in Quotations Page, "Quotations by Author Jerry Falwell." www.quotationspage.com.
14. Furstenberg, *Destinies of the Disadvantaged*, p. 21.
15. Quoted in White House, "America's Challenge." http://clinton2.nara.gov.

16. Quoted in Bill Alexander, "Chastity vs. Condoms Mires Clinton Anti-Teen Mom War," SparkAction, January 1, 1997. http://sparkaction.org.

Chapter Two: What Should Schools Teach About Sex?

17. Quoted in Jamel Major, "MCS Board Working to Deal with Pregnancies at Frayser High School," WMC-TV, January 12, 2011. www.wmctv.com.

18. Quoted in Jane Roberts, "Sex Education Prompts Worries in Memphis," *Memphis (TN) Commercial Appeal*, October 2, 2012. www.commercial-appeal.com.

19. Quoted in Lisa Shencker, "Legislature Passes Bill to Let Schools Drop Sex Education," *Salt Lake Tribune*, May 6, 2012. www.sltrib.com.

20. Quoted in Dana Liebelson, "7 States Trying to Gut Sex Ed and Promote Abstinence," *Week*, April 29, 2013. http://theweek.com.

21. Molly Masland, "Carnal Knowledge: The Sex Ed Debate," NBC News. www.nbcnews.com.

22. Quoted in Heather Clark, "Chicago Board of Education Approves Sex Ed for Kindergarteners," Breaking Christian News, March 1, 2013. http://christiannews.net.

23. Debra Hauser, "What They Need to Know at 5, and at 15," *New York Times*, May 7, 2013. www.nytimes.com.

24. Quoted in StayTeen.org, "Did You Learn a Lot from Your School's Sex Ed Program?" www.stayteen.org.

25. Cindy Speegle, personal interview with the author, May 1, 2013.

26. Quoted in Media Education Foundation, "The Purity Myth," 2011. www.mediaed.org.

27. Quoted in ScienceDaily, "9 of 10 Parents Want Their Kids Abstinent," WND, May 8, 2007. www.wnd.com.

28. Nicole, "After Abstinence, Emergency Contraception," Sex, Etc., March 16, 2007. http://sexetc.org.

29. Quoted in Yuri Resetovs, "States with Abstinence-Only Education Have Higher Teen Pregnancy Rates," New Jersey Newsroom, April 11, 2012. www.newjerseynewsroom.com.

30. Quoted in Theresa Tamkins, "Virginity Pledges Don't Mean Much, Study Says," CNN, December 30, 2008. www.cnn.com.

31. Quoted in DoSomething.org, "11 Questions with a Teen Pregnancy Expert." www.dosomething.org.

32. Quoted in Acacia Stevens, "Abstinence Is Foolproof? Think Again," Sex, Etc., September 11, 2012. http://sexetc.org.

33. Quoted in Katherine Kiang, "Childcare and Development Students Try Out Empathy Bellies," *Devils' Advocate*, March 18, 2013. www.hcdevilsadvocate.com.

Chapter Three: Should Teens Have Access to Birth Control?

34. Quoted in Bonnie Rochman, "Half of Teen Moms Don't Use Birth Control—Why That's No Surprise," *Time*, June 20, 2012. http://healthland.time.com.

35. Ana Nogales, "Family Secrets," *Psychology Today*, March 28, 2012. www.psychologytoday.com.

36. Quoted in ProCon.org, "Would Mandatory Parental Notification Laws Regarding Contraceptive Prescriptions Negatively Affect Teenage Girls' Health?," http://aclu.procon.org.

37. Quoted in Debate.org, "Should Teens Be Able to Obtain Birth Control Without Parental Consent?" www.debate.org.

38. Patrick Welsh, "Column: Schools Dispensing Birth Control," *USA Today*, April 12, 2012. http://usatoday30.usatoday.com.

39. Randy Alcorn, "In Condoms We Trust," Eternal Perspective Ministries, January 1, 1994. www.epm.org.

40. Alan Singer, "Distribution of Condoms in the High Schools," Angel Fire. http://people.hofstra.edu.

41. Natalie Rella, "For Me, Visit to Planned Parenthood Was Positive, Healthy Step," *Tampa Bay Times*, March 5, 2012. www.tampabay.com.

42. Quoted in Bonnie Miller Rubin, "Questions Linger on Plan B," *Albuquerque Journal*, April 29, 2013, p. C3.

43. Quoted in Rubin, "Questions Linger on Plan B," p. C3.

44. Quoted in StayTeen.org, "Did You Learn a Lot from Your School's Sex Ed Program?"

Chapter Four: How Does the Media Influence Teen Pregnancy?

45. Jane D. Brown, ed., *Managing the Media Monster: The Influence of the Media (from Television to Text Messages) on Teen Sexual Behavior and Attitudes*. Washington, DC: National Campaign to Prevent Teen and Unplanned Pregnancy, 2008, p. 4.

46. Gaby Rodriguez, *The Pregnancy Project*. New York: Simon & Schuster, 2012, pp. 133–34.

47. Quoted in Divine Caroline, "Does Media Affect Teen Pregnancy?," www.divinecaroline.com.

48. Quoted in *Talk of the Nation*, "Does Reality TV Misrepresent Teen Parenthood?," August 26, 2011. www.npr.org.

49. Victor C. Strasburger, "Sexuality, Contraception, and the Media," *Pediatrics Digest*, September 1, 2010. www.pediatricsdigest.mobi.

50. Quoted in *Talk of the Nation*, "Does Reality TV Misrepresent Teen Parenthood?"

51. Quoted in Brown, *Managing the Media Monster*, p. 26.

52. Quoted in ScienceDaily, "Songs About Sex—How They Affect Kids: Study Questions the Impact of Sexualized Lyrics on Adolescent Behaviors and Attitudes," September 6, 2011. www.sciencedaily.com.

53. Quoted in Stuart Wolpert, "Teenagers Find Information About Sex on the Internet When They Look for It—and When They Don't, UCLA's Children's Digital Media Center Reports," UCLA Newsroom, January 27, 2005. http://newsroom.ucla.edu.

54. Brown, *Managing the Media Monster*, p. 31.

55. Nicole Chisolm, "We Have the Tools to Reduce Teen Pregnancy," *Advocates' Blog.* www.advocatesforyouth.org.

56. Quoted in MSN News, "Eye-Catching Chicago PSA Stars Pregnant Teen Boys," June 10, 2013. http://news.msn.com.

57. NYC Human Resources Administration, "Think Being a Teen Parent Won't Cost You?" www.nyc.gov.

58. Quoted in Michelle Castillo, "New York City's New Teen Pregnancy PSAs Use Crying Babies to Send Message," CBS News, March 4, 2013. www.cbsnews.com.

Chapter Five: What Else Can Be Done to Reduce Teen Pregnancy?

59. Rodriguez, *The Pregnancy Project,* p. 60.

60. Lisa Covitch, *The Epidemic of Teen Pregnancy: An American Tragedy.* Pittsburgh: Rose Dog, 2012, p. 27.

61. Quoted in National Clearinghouse on Families and Youth, "Podcast Transcript: Michael Carrera." http://ncfy.acf.hhs.gov.

62. Quoted in Children's Aid Society, "Alumni Profile: Sugey Palomares." http://stopteenpregnancy.childrensaidsociety.org.

63. Quoted in Miriam Zoila Perez, "Teen Moms Look for Support, but Find Only Shame," *Colorlines,* May 26, 2011. http://colorlines.com.

64. Quoted in Feminist Women's Health Center, "Teens Talk About Preventing Teen Pregnancy." www.fwhc.org.

65. Quoted in *L.A. Youth,* "Teens Talk About Sex," February 2004. www.layouth.com.

66. Quoted in Feminist Women's Health Center, "Teens Talk About Preventing Teen Pregnancy."

67. Melissa Havard, "Talking to Your Kids About, Ahem, You Know What (S.E.X.)," Advocates for Youth. www.advocatesforyouth.org.

68. Havard, "Talking to Your Kids About, Ahem, You Know What (S.E.X.)."

69. Quoted in *Washington Post*, "In Western Europe," May 16, 2006. www.washingtonpost.com.

70. Advocates for Youth, "Adolescent Sexual Health in Europe and the US," 2011. www.advocatesforyouth.org.

71. Quoted in *Washington Post*, "In Western Europe."

Related Organizations and Websites

Advocates for Youth

2000 M St. NW, Suite 750
Washington, DC 20036
phone: (202) 419-3420
fax: (202) 419-1448
website: www.advocatesforyouth.org

Advocates for Youth works to help young people make informed decisions about reproductive and sexual health through sexual education. The website provides information and statistics about condoms and contraceptives, abstinence, sex education, and European pregnancy prevention strategies, among other data.

Campaign for Our Children, Inc. (CFOC)

One N. Charles St., 11th Floor
Baltimore, MD 21201
phone: (410) 576-9015
fax: (410) 752-7075
website: www.cfoc.org

The CFOC works to inform and educate the public about teen pregnancy prevention. The organization's materials are used throughout the world in teen pregnancy prevention programs. Visitors to the CFOC website can access information about abstinence, talking to parents about sex, sex issues, and links to dozens of informative websites on teen sexual health issues.

Centers for Disease Control and Prevention (CDC)

4770 Buford Hwy.
Atlanta, GA 30341-3717
phone: (800) 232-4636
website: www.cdc.gov

The CDC is the federal government's main public health agency. It offers information on a wide range of public health issues. By typing *teen pregnancy* in the website's search tab, visitors gain access to information, reports, articles, and statistics on teen pregnancy and teen pregnancy prevention programs.

Family Research Council (FRC)

801 G St. NW
Washington, DC 20001
phone: (800) 225-4008
e-mail: corrdept@frc.org
website: www.frc.org

The FRC supports abstinence-based sex education. It opposes condom distribution in schools and allowing minors access to contraceptives without parental involvement. Visitors to the website can access research and reports on abstinence education, the dangers of casual sex, and adolescent health and sexual activity.

Focus on the Family

8605 Explorer Dr.
Colorado Springs, CO 80995
phone: (800) 232-6459
e-mail: help@FocusontheFamily.com
website: www.fotf.org

Focus on the Family is a conservative organization that promotes abstinence-based sex education, abstinence until marriage, and adoption and is opposed to emergency contraceptives. Visitors to the website gain access to information about abstinence education, abstinence until marriage, media decency, and concerns about pornography.

Guttmacher Institute

125 Maiden Ln., 7th Floor
New York, NY 10038
phone: (800) 355-0244
fax: (212) 248-1951
website: www.guttmacher.org

The Guttmacher Institute is devoted to protecting and increasing men's and women's access to services and information involving reproductive health. The institute sponsors many studies and surveys on teen sexuality issues, which can be accessed by following the "Adolescents" link on the institute's website.

Healthy Teen Network

509 Second St. NE
Washington, DC 20002
phone: (202) 547-8814
website: www.healthyteennetwork.org

The Healthy Teen Network is a national organization focused on teen health, teen pregnancy prevention, and supporting teen parents. By clicking on the "Research and Resources" button on the organization's webpage, visitors gain access to information about teen pregnancy prevention, comprehensive sex education, STIs, and adolescent health services.

Heritage Foundation

214 Massachusetts Ave. NE
Washington, DC 20002
phone: (202) 546-4400
e-mail: info@heritage.org
website: www.heritage.org

The Heritage Foundation is a conservative research institute. By clicking on "Issues" on the website's home page, then clicking on "Sex Education and Abstinence," visitors to the website gain access to reports, articles, commentary, and audiotapes on abstinence education, teen sexual behavior and choices, and the debate between abstinence education and comprehensive sex education.

National Abstinence Education Association (NAEA)

1701 Pennsylvania Ave. NW, Suite 300
Washington, DC 20006
phone: (202) 248-5420
fax: (866) 935-4850
e-mail: info@theNAEA.org
website: www.abstinenceassociation.org

The NAEA lobbies Congress and state legislatures to fund abstinence-based education programs. Hot topics on the association's home page include a report on teen pregnancy rates and the effectiveness of abstinence-based education. Visitors to the website can find information about the organization's sex education policies and those of the Obama administration.

National Campaign to Prevent Teen and Unplanned Pregnancy (NCPTUP)

1776 Massachusetts Ave. NW, Suite 200
Washington, DC 20036
phone: (202) 478-8500
fax: (202) 478-8588
website: www.thenationalcampaign.org

The NCPTUP is dedicated to reducing teen pregnancy rates by promoting comprehensive sex education and access to contraception. The organization sponsors media campaigns and surveys and publishes reports and informational booklets. State-by-state statistics on teen pregnancy are also available on the website.

Planned Parenthood Federation of America

434 W. Thirty-Third St.
New York, NY 10001
phone: (212) 541-7800
fax: (212) 245-1845
website: www.plannedparenthood.org

Planned Parenthood is the largest sexual and reproductive health care provider in the United States. It operates more than eight hundred clinics across the country that provide confidential contraceptive services no matter the patient's age or ability to pay. The website provides information about all methods of birth control.

Sexuality Information and Education Council of the United States (SIECUS)

90 John St., Suite 402
New York, NY 10038
phone: (212) 819-9770
fax: (212) 819-9776
e-mail: pmalone@seicus.org
website: www.siecus.org

SIECUS supports an adolescent's right to make responsible sexual choices. It promotes comprehensive sexual education, access to reproductive health services, and STI prevention. Visitors to the website can access fact sheets and information on teen sexuality, teen pregnancy, sex education programs, sexual and reproductive health, and international topics.

Additional Reading

Books

Tamara Campbell and Tamara Orr, *Frequently Asked Questions About Teen Pregnancy*. New York: Rosen, 2011.

Lauri S. Friedman, ed., *Writing the Critical Essay: Teen Pregnancy*. Farmington Hills, MI: Greenhaven, 2010.

Letizia Guglielmo, ed., *MTV and Teen Pregnancy: Critical Essays on "16 and Pregnant" and "Teen Mom."* Lanham, MD: Scarecrow, 2013.

Mary Lane Kamberg, *Teen Pregnancy and Motherhood*. New York: Rosen, 2012.

Lisa Krueger, ed., *Teen Pregnancy and Parenting*. Farmington Hills, MI: Greenhaven, 2011.

Hal Marcovitz, *How Should Sex Education Be Taught in Schools?* San Diego: ReferencePoint, 2013.

Peggy J. Parks, *Teenage Sex and Pregnancy*. San Diego: Reference-Point, 2011.

Periodicals

Jackie Alexander, "More Emphasis Needed on Preventing Teen Pregnancies, Officials Say," *Gainesville (FL) Sun*, March 13, 2012.

Meeri Kim, "Questions About the Effects of Over-the-Counter Plan B for All Ages," *Washington Post*, June 29, 2013.

Mike Stobbe, "Nearly All US States See Hefty Drop in Teen Births," *Las Cruces (NM) Sun News*, May 24, 2013.

Kim Tranell, "The Sex Files: What's Really Going on Behind the Braggy Stories and Totally Racy Rumors? *Seventeen* Talked to Recent Grads to Find Out What They've Learned About Hooking Up in High School—and Wish Every Teen Girl (Like You) Knew," *Seventeen*, August 2012.

Internet Sources

National Public Radio, "Sex Education in America: An NPR/Kaiser/Kennedy School Poll." www.npr.org/templates/story/story.php?storyId=1622610.

Sex, Etc., "Info Center: Stories." http://sexetc.org/sex-ed/info-center/ stories/ #?pageNum=1&topic%5B%5D=stories-birth-control&topic%5B%5D=stories-pregnancy.

StayTeen.org, "Birth Control Explorer." www.stayteen.org/birth-control-101.

TeenHelp.com, "Teen Pregnancy Statistics." www.teenhelp.com/teen-pregnancy/teen-pregnancy-statistics.html.

Index

Picture Credits

About the Author

Barbara Sheen is the author of more than eighty books for young people. She lives in New Mexico with her family. In her spare time, she likes to swim, cook, garden, and walk.